T|

by

Shawn Bailey

Thrifty Scribe, LLC

2

Thrifty Scribe, LLC
212 W. Troy St., STE B
Dothan, AL 36303

First Edition: March 2025
Printed in Dothan, AL US

ISBN 979-8-9859847-4-3

Edited by Evelyn Cammon
Cover illustration by Olegg Kulay-Kulaychuk

1 3 5 7 9 10 8 6 4 2

This book is dedicated to the filthy rich. We're coming for you.

Introduction

The definition of insanity, I'm sure you've heard, is doing the same thing over and over and expecting different results. Yet we do this every day.

We roll out of bed onto a hamster wheel.
We are paid just enough to exist.
We are told we can be anything we want.
We make the rich richer.
We stare at screens to distract from reality.
We go to sleep.
We roll out of bed onto a hamster wheel.

We know this is not how we should count down our precious hours in our short time here. So, we find distractions. To me, insanity is not being able to distract oneself from this repetitive and exhausting reality. Our distractions, however, have devolved to the same level of madness that underpins our existential fears. This appears to be a cruel mobius of dependency from which I believe there is no escape.

Enjoy.

Sir, What's in the Towel?

Tad was writing in front of his apartment window. He was twenty minutes down a rabbit hole before switching tabs to his poem. He was close to having enough poetry to publish a small but respectable chapbook. He figured he was ten pages away from reaching the one seventy mark. You felt like you were holding a book at one seventy. Fewer pages and you felt like you were holding a pamphlet, something people gave out for free on the sidewalk, not demanded sixteen dollars for in a bookstore.

He was three months out of college with no job offers but convinced of the possibility that a book of poetry, if it sold at least two hundred copies, could float his side of the rent for a few months. He'd gathered all his poems together from papers, blogs, contests, forgotten thumb drives, and spiral notebooks dating back to eighth grade. Tad gleaned a hundred twenty pages from a decade of spurious epiphanies. He'd written ten poems in the last month and was halfway through a poem about death and estate sales. He was close to wrapping things up.

But after six years in college, Tad was mentally exhausted. And writing requires thinking and thinking is hard, while activities that facilitate procrastination require very little thought. And there are *so* many ways to procrastinate.

Tad headed to his bathroom with phone in hand. Instagram was first as it seemed the least toxic. Next was Reddit, which could be levelheaded at times. He finished scrolling and set his phone on the sink. This was taking longer than he wanted, but he had learned to take things easier as of late. Everything was always so harried nowadays, and this was something you shouldn't rush. If it was coming, it would come. There was no sense in straining like you were giving birth. That's how you ended up pinching a pasty one in half and leaving the other loaf in the oven. You didn't want it poking its head out in the middle of your day. Or maybe you have to go wipe again at inopportune times. Or feel the liminal wrongness of it every time you take a step.

Tad sat and waited. And waited and waited and waited. He checked out Instagram again and somehow spilled over into YouTube and made the mistake of accidentally catching the latest news. Then he did the childbirth straining anyway because his legs were falling asleep. He ran his hands under his little belly-fat rolls and moved them around, messaging his insides to get things rolling. Then he bent over and pushed. Then he tried sitting up with the posture of a librarian and moved his toes into ballerina position. He'd read somewhere this had something to do with our ancestors and the position we evolved to for pooping. Finally, he leaned back and swayed from side to side like a cobra in front of a metronome.

It was finally moving, but so, so slowly. He leaned forward again and strained to the point he worried about an aneurysm. *Isn't that when a brain vessel pops or something? How many people have died on the pot?* What if they found him beside his toilet in a week, bloated, with a stubborn turd still poking halfway out of his asshole? But it was already in the anal canal. He couldn't let up now, or it would slide back in there. So gross. I mean, it's gross anyway, but once it tastes daylight, letting it back in is unthinkable.

Tad used muscles he didn't know men had, and eventually, he felt a tiny iron cannonball leave him.

"Jesus, Fucking, Christ!" he said to the hot water heater sitting in the corner.

Then Tad Gruber looked down between his legs to survey his work, such as men do. There was the tiniest red cloud in there, which wasn't the first time and wouldn't be the last. All's fair in love and war and pooping.

But there wasn't a brown marble at the bottom of the porcelain. This was something else. It was in the curve, about to slide back into the shadows.

It was a... chrysalis. Yes, that was the word.

Usually unable to find the right word, he amazed himself at his sudden intellectual acuity. But there was no time for celebration as it moved slightly. Tad screamed.

"Wha-! Holyshitwhatthefuck!"

He felt like he should run, but that didn't make sense under the circumstances. He had to know what was going on because this thing... this thing just came out of him. Whatever this was had been *inside* him. He shivered involuntarily, wiped his ass absentmindedly, threw the rag in the trash, and pulled his pants up hoping he was clean enough.

It moved again.

He looked around. His roommate wasn't home and he needed to verify this event with someone else. His mind going through everything he'd eaten in the last few days. Did something have some sort of eggs in it that hatched inside him?

"Oh, Jesus. Oh, Jesus."

His body was in a stalemate with his brain. And what about stomach acids? Couldn't they eat through almost anything? Wouldn't they have killed it on the way through, or maybe it didn't grow to maturity until it was down in the intestines? Weren't there fruits that could only spread from being digested and pooped out?

Tad grabbed his phone and was about to dial his roommate when the realization hit him that there might still be more of those inside him... squirming around. He closed his eyes and concentrated all his senses on his stomach, butthole, and everything in between. He felt nothing, but then again, he had felt nothing peculiar before this thing popped out of his taint. He looked down at the thing in the bottom of the toilet, then ran to his roommate's bathroom and sat down, immediately squeezing as hard as he could over and over. He did this for about five or so minutes to no avail, stood up, wiped, and ran back to the other toilet. It was still in there. Small movements. Something on the inside, ready to meet the outside world.

Dying occurred to him. If there were thirty or forty of these things inside him, could they hatch and start eating their way out? He ran to the kitchen and slung doors open in a panic. Some kind of plastic container, then way too long to not find the top, grabbing a mason jar, then back to the bathroom. He wasn't reaching down in there. No fucking way. A coat hanger. No. A cup measure or spoon. No. Boom! Running to his bedside, grabbing a back scratcher, fishing it out on the first try. Hell yeah! Into the container. Top on. Wrapped in a towel because, you know, toilet water. He ran to the car. Forgot his keys. Ran back. Trying to keep it only ten miles per hour over the speed limit but knowing only the ER could save him if bad things started happening. He could already be bleeding internally.

He almost rear-ended a hatchback at a red light after staring too long at the wrapped thing in the seat beside him.

Something inside me. Something inside me. Jesus Christ.

He repeated this over and over like it was a Hail Mary. Every food he had put in his mouth in the last three or four days was now suspect. That breakfast biscuit? Those biscuit people come in at like four in the morning. Who supervises them? Anyone? That

Five Layer burrito. Eighty-eight percent beef. Maybe that other twelve percent finally caught up with him. Those frozen pizza bites. Processed. And where? What was the country of origin? Was it USA or Papua New Guinea? Who the fuck knows?

He even pictured his roommate dropping roofies in his beer and then sneaking into his room at night with something he found outside. The newest thing since cow tipping. Boofing insects. Nothing was off the table as far as his paranoid mind was concerned. They say your gut has a mind of its own. What if this thing leaked out something that gave his gut-mind dementia and he started craving raw chicken or pizza with pineapple? What if he had to shit into a bag? His uncle knew a guy who did that. How many gallon-size Ziploc bags would he have to buy each month to shit in? How does that even work? How does it not get all over you when you zip it up? He knew it didn't work like this, but his mind was trying to distract him from the intense panic of knowing that something living was inside him and had been for an unknown period of time. Tad could not stop thinking of eggs. Thousands and thousands of eggs. Adhering to the sides of his intestinal walls and growing larger and larger each minute.

He whipped into the ER and almost pulled up to the door but stopped short and sped around to the parking lot. He wasn't bleeding or in immediate visible danger, so that could cause issues. He found an empty spot, got out, and raced to the front window after passing through the first set of sliding doors.

"How can I help you?" asked the young girl behind the counter.

"I need to see the doc - I um, I um, had something in my poop," Tad said, holding up the bottle wrapped in a towel as proof.

"What?" She leaned back and kept her eye on the towel, except to glance at the guard by the other set of sliding doors that led to the inside of the actual emergency room. Tad could see the man moseying his way over from the corner of his eye. He realized what he must look like waving some object wrapped in a towel while talking excessively fast and trying not to appear panicked. He tried to slow down a little.

"I was taking a poop and looked down—look, there was something in a chrysalis that came out and something may still be in there. I just need an x-ray or something..."

The guard stood behind and to his side.

"Sir," she said with a look that said this wasn't her first rodeo, "do you have an object lodged inside of you?"

Tad waved his hand in a no, no, no fashion. She had said it loud enough for half the ER to hear her. He was sure if he turned around, he would find his entire graduating class filling the seats for assorted reasons, nodding their heads knowingly.

"No, ma'am," he said. "I mean... I mean, I didn't put anything in there." He was leaning over and whispering conspiratorially now. "Something was already in there and—

"Already in there?" Incredulous. Tired of this whacko.

The guard now, "Sir, what's in the towel?"

"It's what was... inside—"

"Sir, do not wave it around," the guard said a little too forcefully.

"I was just showing you what it was," Tad explained as he began unwrapping the towel. The ER hostess now long-eyeing the guard. "...what came out."

As he pulled the last bit of white cotton from around the jar, he could see that the thing was no longer inside the chrysalis. A tan husk lay against the side of the jar in a few droplets of water, a small cesarean split running across it. The lady and guard scrunched up their faces and fumbled for something to say; the guard, needing to assert his dominance over the crazy man with insects, and the lady, needing to not be helpful to whomever stepped foot in front of her, but both were so perplexed by what was in front of them, they were at a loss for words.

It was about four inches long, which was twice the size of the chrysalis. This increased Tad's anxiety a hundred-fold. It looked like a cross between a worm and a baby bee if a baby bee had an exoskeleton that refracted light in blue, red, and purple like oil on water. It's eyes taking up half the head, off to the sides. Little caterpillar legs. Curled in on itself which meant that if it unfurled it would be even larger than it looked now.

"Sir, you need to take that back outside." The guard now over the fleeting novelty of it and more concerned about keeping order, a task that included not letting weird insects get loose in the ER and crawl up someone's pant leg.

"Yes, sir," Tad said, "It's just that I need to show th—"

"Outside with it, now."

Tad could see himself being wrestled to the ground by this man, the glass breaking in the process, and the thing crawling back into his butthole. That was not an option. He relented. Back to the car. Making sure the top was screwed on tight. The thought of it getting loose in the car. Him setting the car on fire. Realizing that when he first parked and went in, he had left the keys dangling in the ignition and being surprised that, in this neighborhood, he had a car still.

Back inside, he found that a guy with a bleeding arm and a whole family that was arguing had gotten in front of him. Jesus fucking Christ. Another 30 minutes added to the ledger. After finally signing in, he waited for two and a half hours before they called him to triage. He explained to the lady taking his vitals what had happened. She gave him a poker face and sent him back to the waiting room. Another forty-five minutes. What will happen, he thought, if I start crying? Three hours to imagine all the different things that could be happening inside of him. His intestines chewed through. His gut sloughing off inside him. If it doubled in size in under an hour, how big would one be after three hours of fucking around on the first floor of this shithole hospital? Jesus fucking Chr—

"Tad Gruber!" the voice rang out.

He jumped up and almost ran to the door, not making eye contact with the guard as he walked by. He was behind the final set of sliding doors at last. Another lady. Him relating the same story. At least he was getting better at articulating the strange and impossible thing that had happened to him. She nodded as if he were the tenth person that day with ass worms. "Why of course, sir, I'll fetch my ass worm tools and we'll go to work."

"Just disrobe and put this on and I'll be back in a sec," which she was, and with what looked like a doctor or surgeon.

They laid him over on his side and he felt something cold and jelly-like being rubbed on his butt and then, boom, the doctor sliding something in there without even asking. No first date or anything and this doctor was at fourth base already. Then the pressure releasing.

"Don't see anything right off, Mr. Gruber. What did you say it was again?"

The nurse whispering to the doctor.

"I know what it sounds like, but it was a chrysalis. What was inside me has hatched and is in a jar in my car."

The doctor said, "Okay, let's get an x-ray and go from there." His footsteps disappearing into the hall with every word. The jelly, having been applied like sloppy joe on a prison bun, was running everywhere.

He asked for a towel and got three paper towels, which did about as well removing the gel as you'd think. After the nurse left, he had to retrieve more himself, then squat down and wipe himself next to his bed. God knows who was listening on the other side of the curtain.

Another thirty minutes and they finally took him to x-ray, got some glamour shots of his belly and groin area, then dropped him off at his room of curtains. *This is some one-off thing, he consoled himself. Some weird, but explainable happenstance that occurred naturally and had actually happened to other people that he had simply never heard of.* This is what Tad Gruber told himself until the doctor came in and said,

"Sir, you have some sort of mass growing inside you. I've sent this to as many colleagues as I could and they've never seen anything like it."

"Wha— What? Are you messing with me?" Tad looking from the nurse to the doctor. The doctor holding up the x-ray. He could see his spine, hip bones, and a shadowy, spider-webby blob over the right hip bone. "What in the hell is it?" he asked, his hand moving to the spot on his body.

The doctor said, "We're not sure. We'd like to do a colonoscopy."

Tad stared at them.

"Right now," the doctor clarified. "Is that okay with you?"

He thought he should call his mom. But what would he say?

"Yes," he answered. "Will, will I be out?"

"Yes."

"And you guys can get it out?" Tad said, staring at the thick, black-and-white image that the doc was now holding by his side.

"Well, we need to see what we're working with first, but at the least, there'll be a biopsy."

Tad said, "Um, okay." I mean, what could he say?

He looked down at the skin covering that spot and then imagined that thing just a few inches under it. Cancer didn't come to mind. Tumors don't spit out insects.

That thing.

In his car.

In the heat.

With the lid sealed tight and no oxygen. It would die soon if it hadn't already. Good. They can give it to an insectologist, or whatever you call those people, and they can figure out what it is and where it came from. Maybe some idiot brought it from another country. There were alligators in the river down from his place, not because the environment was suited to them or because it was their natural habitat, but because about a decade ago, some idiot from Florida had dumped some of their exotic pet overflow into the edge of the water. The gators never bothered anybody swimming or skiing, but you wouldn't take your chihuahua out to poop by the water's edge. That's all it was, Tad told himself. Some idiot from Florida.

He thought there would be hours more of waiting, but the nurse was already clicking buttons and handles on his bed and swiveling him around to exit the room. This was too much. Too fast. But there was nothing else he could do. The doctors simply needed to get it the hell out of him.

They rolled him straight to the surgery room. Everything about twenty degrees colder. Nurses placating him with smiles and empty words. He could hear the concern and lack of certainty in the doctors' conversations. Lights above him. Then counting backward. Then—

A Myriad of Diverse Violations

He came to, abruptly. There was no swimming around in the subconscious for a few fuzzy minutes. He was knocked out and then wide awake. He could feel them inside him. All kinds of shit inside him today. A myriad of diverse violations. Did they not see that he was awake? Wasn't the anesthesiologist usually all over that?

"There it is, guys," one of them said.

Tad could see no one. They were all behind him, digging around in his butt with a camera.

"Oh, my. Look at the colors," another said.

A woman full of amazement exclaimed, "Holy shit. That looks like an octopus crossed with a—"

"Oooooohhhhhhh!" A collective gasp. People stepping back.

"Rrrruuuuttt?" Tad tried to say.

"Oh, shit. He's awake," someone said.

Someone next to him. Tad screaming, but only on the inside. Thinking of the Rolling Stones because of that song. What was that song agai—

Subsonic Chipmunks

Wide awake once again. Something he was certain was not supposed to happen. Looking around the room, he spotted a nurse undoing a package or needle or something. She turned to him and let out a short, muffled scream. She didn't even bother walking out of the room, just hollered, "He's awake," then stood there until the doctors came. And that was something different. Before there was one fairly disinterested doctor. Now there were six doctors. They motioned for the nurse to leave, which she did with haste.

"Mr. Gruber, you back with us?" one said.

"Fully," he said, noticing that he suddenly had a strange craving for shrimp. Strange because even the smell of seafood triggered his gag reflex. Remembering this, he gagged.

One of the doctors, who were all wearing masks and gloves, handed him a small banana-shaped container to throw up in.

"You okay?"

Tad said, "Fine."

He was most certainly not fine. He should be on his couch, streaming a movie while slowly sipping a beer. Instead, he was surrounded by a cadre of surgeons. At least, that's the word that came into his mind for a group of doctors. He would look this up later.

"Well," another one said, "We won't beat around the bush." He held up the second X-ray he'd seen that day. It had a mass on it similar to the earlier one, but now it was further up and over. Tad became transfixed. Another voice from the crowd said what he was thinking.

"It moved."

Another said, "We got a small biopsy, but as soon as we snipped it, that thing took off like it was in a race."

Tad's face was as drawn into itself as one's face can get. You can only show so much concern. Then it's just screaming.

"The fuck is in me, guys?"

A mask said, "Everyone has their theories. A fast-moving parasite, a cephalopod, something alien. We're not certain what the hell it is."

Tad said nothing. Did not move.

"We tried ultrasound while you were out, but it seems to pick up on the waves and moves to another part of your tract. We also started a capsule endoscopy. Little pill with a camera. Should be seeing something in 8 to 12 hours. You're wearing the monitor. We'd like to do a PET scan to maybe assess the metabolic activity of... well, whatever it might be."

Tad remained motionless. He could see they were all very, very curious. They were wondering what tools they had that could poke and prod and send radioactive energy through him. They were like a group of middle-grade boys on the side of the riverbank, poking the bloated beaver to see if it would explode.

Tad was thinking of a big truck with a superpowered vacuum hose attached to it. He'd heard about these things being shoved into holes in someone's yard and it sucking out chipmunks and gophers at subsonic speeds into the back of a truck. He was picturing himself in the middle of someone's yard, on his knees, face to the lush grass, as a matter-of-fact guy in a yellow helmet reached down and shoved that oversized hose where the sun don't shine. That's what he needed. Not these people.

Tad didn't trust doctors. They used to try and cure you with arsenic and leeches. He was already projecting himself into one of those 19th-century-looking surgery rooms as these doctors pointed at his pale body on a cold slab. They address the students behind the glass above them. *And of course, you can see here where the cephalopod exploded from his anus when we began the PET scan...*

It was too much. Tad asked for the rails to be lowered and then slid off and walked over to the chair. He realized then that he wasn't in the ER, but had his own room. He picked up his pants and began to put them on.

"Um, Tad. Sir, it's very important that we see what's going on in there. That... that thing is the size of your fist and is moving very quickly to be inside one of your major organs."

Tad put on his shirt and grabbed his shoes. He didn't try to put his socks over the socks they had placed on him.

"Mr. Gruber?"

Fully dressed now, Tad stood before the group of doctors. He was so hungry. He thought about shrimp and grits and gagged loudly. They all took a step back. When he walked forward, they parted like the Red Sea.

Buffalo Wings and Bleach

Tad walked through the ER parking lot like a tranquilized zombie. It was nighttime, but he had no idea what the exact time was. He opened his car door. The ceiling of the car cast its dim light on the mason jar in the passenger seat. Still there. He slid into his seat, aware that he was not the least bit sore from whatever procedures had taken place. That thing, probably. Didn't some bugs secrete something to deaden the flesh where they were doing their dirty work on you? Maybe this thing was doing that to his insides. Jesus Christ. Something was inside him. *Inside* him.

But there was good news. As the ceiling light went out, he pressed the button to illuminate the front seats. The worm was no more. The only thing left was a dried-out husk. The leftover, brownish outer layer was semitransparent, so he could see that it was hollow. There was nothing else in the jar. Good. That motherfucker dried out from the heat, trapped in the car. Heat. Heat is what kills this thing. Maybe that was its Achilles heel, like cold was for the Blob.

Tad cranked the car, didn't look behind him, and pulled out. He had a plan now. His phone was at fifteen percent when he thumbed it. Ravi answered, surrounded by a din of background noise. A party or bar. Ravi was extroverted. Ravi had friends. This irritated Tad, but only slightly, because whenever he felt like it, Ravi always welcomed him on nightly excursions. Hours of human interaction, with all the expectations and rollercoasters of emotions, drained Tad. So, he enjoyed time to himself with movies and drinks and popcorn that felt like glass in his belly later.

"Hey, I need you to come back to the apartment, like right now. I've been to the hospital. Need someone to watch me if I fall asleep."

He had to repeat himself several times, yelling into the phone, certain at one point that Ravi was feigning deafness in order to not leave whatever party he was at.

Tad said, "Dude, this is serious. Not a joke. Please come now."

The next call was to a local restaurant whose specialty was beer and wings. This is when he found out what time it was. The girl on the other end said, "Let me check if the kitchen is still going." When she came back with an affirmative, Tad ordered forty of their hottest, extra crispy and wet. It was twenty 'til eleven. Tad picked up his order at the bar and tipped the girl a twenty. He then drove to Walmart and left with a container of bleach.

His phone was at seven percent when it rang. It was Ravi.

"The fuck are you, dude? You sound like you just had open heart surgery and then you're not even here." Voices in the background. Not good. He didn't need company. He needed a witness that would believe him.

Tad said, "Sorry. Almost ther—," and the phone went dead. No matter. He was only minutes out. But as if his body was aware of this, he felt something—a pressure, a movement, a ball of expectation in his stomach. Stick to the plan, he thought. Stick to the plan.

Tad came through the door like a freight train, plastic bags full of wings and bleach in tow.

"Dude, what the—" Ravi was saying. Two girls in the room with him, drinking. They were both hot.

"Is your phone charged?" Tad asked, setting the wings on the counter. "Awesome! Follow me to the bathroom and get ready to record." From the corner of his eye, he could see everybody giving each other looks.

Then he heard one of the girls say, "Oh, man. I gotta see this!"

Tad turned the bath faucet on and stopped the tub, then he opened the bleach and as Ravi and the two girls filed into the tiny bathroom, he poured a few capfuls of bleach into the water. He'd worked prep at a restaurant a few years ago and knew that a little went a long way in killing things. They would add a capful to the large sink full of Romaine lettuce and wash it before using. Too much, though, and bad things could start happening to your skin and body. He used six capfuls, hoping he'd gauged it correctly.

Tad opened the bottom drawer of his portable containers and pulled out a stool softener, taking a giant swig. Everyone watched in silence as he placed the bottle on the sink and sat on the edge of the tub. They stared at each other.

Ravi crooked his head expectantly, "Dude?"

"Sorry," Tad said, "Oh, one sec."

He squeezed past them and returned with the Styrofoam container of wings and the mason jar. He lay the jar with the husk on its side in the sink and sat on the tub again. He flipped open the wings and began eating.

They all had beers and took a drink together. One girl said, "Dude, are you okay?"

Talking around his chicken, Tad said, "No. Not at all. Not sure if you want to hear this ladies, but I've been to the hospital today. And I know what this sounds like, but this is not a joke. I'm dead fucking serious right now."

"O-Kay," said Ravi. "What's going on?"

"Took a shit earlier, at least that's what I thought I was doing. Actually pooped out a chrysalis, and yes, it's just like you're imagining it. No idea why or how. I haven't eaten any kind of exotic food. Just the normal shit. Anyway, I freaked out, put it in that jar." They all looked at the jar in the sink and back at him. "Something goddamn hatched out of it on the way there. Worm-like, baby caterpillar-looking shit." He was on his fifth wing already. "And they dug around

in my butt and I have a camera capsule inside me and
_"

They didn't believe him. Tad didn't bother with cleaning his hands, setting the wings over on the closed toilet and pulling off his shirt. After all this, he was aware that he wasn't in as good of shape as he should be at twenty-five. College had added about thirty pounds over the course of five and half years. But they could see the monitor now. Incredulity transforming into a lesser doubt.

"There's something alive and moving around inside me. Moved when they took a biopsy. Whatever laid that fucking thing inside of me is still in there. I gotta get it the fuck out."

The brunette, "Why didn't you let the doctors do their thing?"

"I did! They had no idea what the fuck it was and were about to start trial and erroring on me. No fucking way." Tad, back to eating, was on his eighth wing. "When I went in there, I was just another body and when I left, there were like eight doctors in my room. I'm not shitting you guys."

They were silent while Tad finished his last wing and the water crept slowly up the sides of the tub. It was three or four inches deep.

The dirty blonde, more doubtful than the brunette, who had obviously had a few more than her friend, said, "So, um, what's the plan."

Tad picked up his shirt and wiped his hands on it. His nose was running now and his eyes watering. He didn't look well, or sane for that matter, but he was keenly aware of this.

"I need you to film," waving his hands around, "or get me set up to film... me pooping again. I know what it sounds like, but the heat killed this thing, so I think heat," pointing to the empty to-go container on the bathroom floor, "is how we kill it."

Silence. Staring. Raised eyebrows.

Tad said, "Dude, I'm so serious right now. I'll pay you!"

"I am not goin—" Ravi started to say.

The dirty blonde, "How much?" Her friend smothering a drunken laugh.

Ravi saying, "Jesus, Tad. This is a new level of literal party pooping."

Everyone laughing at this, even Tad, who said, "I'll pay you a hundred dollars to film it proper."

The blonde smiling. "Make it two hundred."

Tad starting to answer when her friend said, "I'll do it for free."

Everyone looked at her, her friend jabbing her in the arm for screwing them out of a possible two hundred dollars.

"I've gotta see this shit!" she explained. Everyone shaking their heads.

Tad's stomach rolling. Ravi picking up the jar from the sink. The brunette saying she was almost ready, tapping at her phone. Tad saying she couldn't stream this. Blondie still trying to negotiate for a hundred. Ravi turning the jar around to inspect the husk. The brunette saying, "she's recording now." Blondie trying to get her phone going as well. Tad saying if they give up the video as soon as they're done, he'll CashApp a hundred bucks. Ravi with the unscrewed lid to the jar in his hands, getting a better look at what was inside. The brunette asking what that is stuck to the underside of the lid that no one else saw. Tad screaming.

First Edition

Ravi threw the lid and the jar into the sink where it cracked into a few large pieces, the lid resting on top of the shards.

"Jesus Christ, did you touch it, Ravi?" Tad hollered.

"Holy shit, dude. You scared the shit outta me."

The girls laughing. Ravi checking his hand. Did he touch it? All of them leaning over the sink to see the thing attached to the lid, but the lid, of course, was turned over.

Tad reached out and carefully turned it over before dropping it back into the glass shards. Yes, there was something there. Green and sticky. About three inches. Something square-looking up under the goop.

"What is that?" the blonde said, the brunette filming everything. "Something's under the boogery stuff."

Ravi, not to be outdone, reaching out himself and grabbing a clear shard from the jar. He drew it across the edge of one side, trying to not cut whatever was under the film, and then sliced the adjacent side. It flipped over before they could even jump back. A collective gasp as they realized it was only the tension from the rubbery gloop, snapping to one side and flipping the object over.

"That looks..."

"Like a..."

"Book."

"Dude," Ravi said, "Is that the back? Looks like writing."

The blonde running back into the living room and reemerging with a little zip-lock-looking purse. She produced a set of tweezers and held them out for whomever. "I ain't touching that thing."

The brunette saying she'll do it. Taking the tweezers and sliding them in between the other side of the goop and the tiny object. She pulled, stopping a couple of times to make sure the tension didn't snap the whole thing toward her. It finally released and she held it up, but the tweezers were obfuscating the other side. She took a few steps and released it, other side up, on the top of the toilet lid.

A title. A tiny image. An author's name, maybe?

"Dude, that's a tiny ass book. Are you screwing with us right now?" Ravi and the girls looked at Tad.

"No," he said flatly, grabbing his toothbrush from the sink. "Grab onto the side, he said to the brunette."

As she did, he pressed on the other side with the toothbrush. The tiny pages separated. A microcosm of words filled the pages. Words so small no one could make them out. Except the title, which was the largest of the print anywhere on the outside. It looked like two-point font, but you could make it out.

The Fairy in the Orchid.

Barbarians at the Gate

"Guys, I have to poop."

The blonde said, "This is very interesting in a prankish, weird way, but, um, I'm going to grab another beer and hang out in the living room until, uh, you know, you're all done with this part. Mind if I take the mini-book to look at?"

No one objected. Ravi didn't want to lose the momentum he had with the blonde, but there was a miniature book sitting on the toilet that his roomie said came out of his butt. He'd always thought the phrase "Bros before hoes" was for misogynistic idiots, but he supposed it kind of made sense in this particular situation. He would stay for now.

"I'm still recording," said the brunette smiling, "Let's get this sideshow going."

Up until this point, Tad had other things on his mind, like some sort of octopus face-hugger swimming around in his intestines, to pay attention to other, novel concerns. But as he turned the faucet off and pulled his pants down, he was keenly aware that he was about to be exposed, and not just to a fairly hot girl, but possibly the entire world if this got out. Two guys and a tub. He could already see the title.

But his phone was dead. He thought about asking her not to record; Ravi had his phone out and ready, and that was enough. But her smile caught him off guard. His pants in a bunch on the tile, he stepped into the water in his underwear.

He said to Ravi, "Throw a towel down would you?"

There was a moment of hesitation and then Tad could feel the barbarians at the gate. Something happening at the event horizon. Maybe the wings worked. Maybe it would come out. He pulled the back of his underwear down, but not the front, squatted, and let nature take its course. He didn't have to push. It plopped right out. Tad didn't wipe. Simply pulled his underwear up and stepped out of the tub onto the towel.

Ravi, the brunette, and Tad all stared at what was submerged and resting on the bottom of the tub. It lay there, inert, for a good thirty seconds before Ravi spoke up.

"Dude, that's just a turd."

The Book Thief

Tad left the main bathroom and went to his tiny, bathless version. He grabbed the back scratcher that was propped up in the corner next to the plunger. He took it back to the tub and pressed the little metal protrusions into the turd. The water was already fading to brown, and this made it worse. He shoved it down every inch or so until he had sliced the turd into several pieces. The water a brown soup now. The brunette stopped recording. She brought her bottom lip up. Shucks, it seemed to say. I thought we would see an alien or something.

"Dude," Ravi said, "are you okay, brother?"

No. Tad was not okay. The brunette turning her phone around. The video in the process of deletion. Tad didn't know what to say next. How do you recover from shitting in your bathtub and then stirring the piece of shit around in it? Ravi told him they were going to hang out in the living room if he wanted to clean up and join them, a genuine look of concern on his face.

After ten minutes of sitting alone in his room, Tad's phone rang. Regional Medical Center. He unplugged it and ran into the living room. Everyone whispering. Great. He waved his hands to get their attention and then made the international symbol known by librarians everywhere. Shush! Tad turned his phone around to show them who was calling and then answered on speaker phone.

"Hello?"

"Hi. This is doctor Milnerd from the hospital. Is this Mr. Gruber?" the doctor asked.

"Yes."

"Okay. I realized earlier that we ganged up on you a little and it may have been overwhelming. I apologize for that. But we do have your best interest at heart. We're checking to see if you're okay."

"Um, no. I have some sort of alien octopus in my ass that won't come out. And it's laying things in there that are alive."

"Yes. About that, do you still have that in the jar?" Milnerd asked.

That follow up question seemed a little off center to Tad. Like they were more interested in the thing that came out than him.

"Yeah. Let's get back to the thing that's living inside of me. What did you and the fellows think of that?"

The tiny crowd in his living room showing renewed interest.

"Well, that was a little unsettling. When we took the biopsy, and... well, when it moved like it did, yes, that was disconcerting. I know it must be very concerning and you're curious about how we're going to extract it without hurting you. And trust me, that's what we're all concentrating on at the moment. I think we've figured out a way for approaching this in the safest manner possible. Do you think you can come back in an hour or so. We'll have all the necessary doctors and equipment here."

Tad said, "Let me think about it. I'll call you back."

"No problem. This is my persona—" Tad hung up.

"See? I'm not a lunatic. This happened. Something is inside me." He pointed to his stomach. "And it fucking laid a thing that hatched and created—" He looked around. "Where's the book?"

"Oh," said the blonde, taking it out of her pocket and holding it up, "the booty book!"

She was laughing, but Tad wasn't. He glanced at Ravi to show disapproval, then reached out and took the book. *His* book. It came out of *his* ass. Who tries to steal an ass book? Somehow, the mood turned even more awkward.

"Alcohol," said Tad. "Maybe that would affect it?"

Ravi said, "Dude, why don't you just go back to the hospital? If you really have some kind of parasite or something in there, you need to have professionals looking at it, not trying to chase it out with buffalo wings and vodka."

At least Ravi seemed genuinely concerned, but then the blonde gave some kind of eye signal to Ravi and he said, "Just go to the hospital, bro," as he turned and walked to his room, the blonde holding his hand. For a split second, he thought the brunette would stay, but she gave a conciliatory smile and followed them. Awesome.

Tad went to the kitchen and poured vodka into some orange juice. He knew he couldn't handle this himself, but didn't trust the doctors either. Something in their voices; in the way they approached him. He took the mixed drink and the book to his room. He guzzled half the glass then set it down and turned his attention to the book. Using his phone, he took a picture of the cover. Then spread the picture out on his phone with his fingers. He could see the title much easier now and, as he moved the image around, the picture on the front. It was an orchid, and hiding behind one of the leaves, poking its head out, the fairy. *The Fairy in the Orchid.* He moved down to the bottom and read the author's name. He read it several times. Thought about running into Ravi's room and showing them, but then thought better of it. Even considering what had happened so far, he simply could not believe his eyes.

It read: Tad Gruber.

He tried to reconcile this development with reality. With things that he could touch and feel and knew existed. He felt like the dream world had engulfed him and he only needed to wake up. Instead, he fell asleep listening to the muffled moans in the next room.

Shrimp and Grits

Tad woke up like he did in the hospital. Despite having drunk too much the night before, he woke up rested and clearheaded. Sitting up in bed, he closed his eyes, listening intently to his body. He felt fine. His gut wasn't bubbling, and he didn't feel at all sick to his stomach or hungover. He got up and went to the bathroom to brush his teeth, but remembered he'd used his toothbrush to pry open the butt book. *The Fairy in the Orchid*. What a strange, strange little story.

He looked in the mirror. Though he felt one hundred percent, he looked eighty percent. Was he paler than usual? Were his eyes a little darker? He kind of looked like an older version of Oliver Twist, or how he pictured Oliver Twist, anyway. That little English ragamuffin who was covered in dirt and asking for another bowl of porridge, or whatever those Brits ate back then. Wasn't porridge just oatmeal or cornmeal or something? This made him think of grits and then a flash in his mind of shrimp and grits, but not the normal shrimp and grits. This bowl had that reddish roux and the peppers and the grits, but the shrimp weren't that basic size they sell in the seafood departments. They were the raw, heads on, giant fuckers he'd seen on some documentary about the Philippines. They were the size of lobsters. In his mind, he could see three of these raw things, legs working overtime, laid on their side atop the bed of grits and gravy.

"EEgggkk," he gagged. "The fuck!? Get outta my head."

It was the first time Tad thought about the thing in his belly controlling his mind. This led to him giving in and heading back to the hospital. On the way, he thought about things that he normally didn't toss around, like free will and whether or not alien, octopus slime clogged one's arteries. And what if this thing started moving around? Where could it go? He pictured it crawling out of his mouth at night and slithering up his nose and into his brain. It would make him into a travelling sideshow. He would go around telling people there was an alien in his butt and then poop into his travelling bathtub. Again, everyone in his graduating class looking on in disappointment, heads shaking. We always knew Tad would end up a travelling poop spectacle.

When he pulled into the ER parking lot, it was just after nine in the morning. He grabbed his phone to call the doctor when he noticed a couple of doctors already heading his way, waving. They had seen him pull in. They were... waiting for him? Creepy. But he figured what he had was some sort of one in a billion medical phenomenon, so there was maybe money or prestige wrapped up in it somehow. Maybe he would be featured years from now in a documentary on weird medical stuff. And for the first time, he thought, maybe there's some money in it for me.

A Warm Blanket

When Tad entered the ER before, he was the same as any other random person that had the misfortune to call this the nearest emergency room. Now he had more doctors than he could shake a stick at ushering him into the hospital. He walked straight through the waiting room like he was king of some foreign country. How many countries have kings, he wondered as he walked past that guard that gave him stink-eye last time. The guard stared off into the distance like there wasn't a small parade filing through the sliding doors in front of him. He wondered if this was how Justin Timberlake entered the ER. Didn't he rent a whole department store one time? Maybe Tad could rent the hospital out. Get all the warm blankets to himself.

"Can I have a warm blanket?" he said to no one in particular, testing the amount of power he now wielded.

Someone behind him answering, "Of course, Mr. Gruber."

That's right, bitches. Mr. Gruber. Sir Gruber, even.

But instead of going to a room, they led him to one of the doctors' offices where he sat in a nice leather chair while one doctor sat behind a desk and the others stood around him like introverts at a high school dance party.

"Mr. Gruber," said the doctor with a big, wide smile. At least, that's what Tad imagined from his eyes, as the rest of his face was a mask. They were happy to have him and said so. They would get this thing out of him. They would make absolute sure that he was not harmed in the process. They said so. But they did want him to sign some papers saying that if something did happen, well, you know, Tad wouldn't reach into the hospital's deep pockets and pull out some compensation for, I don't know, say, him having to shit in a bag for the rest of his life. Same old bullshit. What choice did he have? What choice do any of us ever have? You either sign what they put in front of you, or you don't move forward; you don't get the service or the product. And you hope that some consumer protection groups catch any heinous things corporations sneak in there.

Tad smiled, signed the papers. Then thought of those prawns. He could see the gray flesh inside the translucent shells.

"EEggkkt." Tad's mouth opened slightly. The doctors all took a step back, adjusting their masks to fully cover their faces.

"Mr. Gruber," the doctor behind the desk asked, "Are you okay? Is there something wrong... you know, other than the obvious?"

Tad didn't know if he should tell them or not.

"Yeah. I keep getting flashes of shrimp and grits. Like I'm craving seafood for, like, a millisecond. Thing is, I hate seafood. The smell of it. Anything. So, it makes me gag."

A few of them shared side glances.

"Shrimp? Hmmm," the doctor said.

The one doing the talking turned and whispered something to another doctor by his side, who promptly ducked out of the group and left.

Putting him in his own private room this time. Bringing him several warm blankets. Leading him down to the surgery room. Telling him to count backward from a hundred. Tad getting into the sixties while the anesthesiologists exchanged heated words. Tad thinking, yeah, I'm going to die on this table today. Tad finally closing his eyes. Coming to in the middle of things, but with everything hazier than before. Tad fairly certain that, in those few seconds, he saw an open bag of shrimp lying on the steel trolley.

Five-O

Tad was immediately awake. He was still in the surgery room, face down. That was strange. He rolled onto his side then sat up. There were several people in the room, some standing and getting care and some on the floor not moving, but all of them covered in blood. And cops. Cops that were very startled at him sitting up like he did. Cops that drew their guns and pointed them at him.

"Don't you fucking move!" one shouted.

Tad did not move.

Skating Rink Strobe Lights

Two cops that were in the hall burst into the room with guns drawn as well. Four guns pointed at him. This was when Tad became aware of his nudity. He was no longer in his gown, weenie flag flying free in front of cops and doctors and nurses and what appeared to be a couple of dead surgeons on the floor.

"What do we do? Like, how the fuck do we handle this?" one cop said to another.

"Give me a sec," said a voice that wanted to sound commanding, but was obviously still figuring things out.

Tad said, "Guys! I'm obviously not armed! Could you please point those somewhere else!?"

They did not. In fact, the looks on their faces seemed to relay the opposite notion. That Tad was the most heavily armed person on the planet, and waving guns around instead of his cold, pale hands. Yes, he thought, it's cold as shit in here.

"Sir?" another policeman asked.

"Just keep your hands in the air," was the reply, cop speaking to him instead of answering the other one's question.

There were more doctors and nurses huddled together next to the door, watching intently. Tad sitting on the table, bright lights illuminating everything. In this freezer of a room, Tad was somehow sweating. Then he heard a scratching noise behind him. Then a squishy slithering noise. Then scratching again. He turned his head slowly, very slowly, because he didn't want another slug in him.

"Hey!" the cops all chimed in. "Don't move, I said!" Louder this time, seasoned with a dash of panic in their wavering voices.

Tad's head was sideways when he saw it. It was headed up the steel bar on the table behind him. It was about the size of his hand and had sea urchin projections one second, hard and sharp and thin, and slimy tentacles the next, suckers with soft, sloppy movements. It was changing colors like a chameleon on cocaine. One second to the next was a kaleidoscope of bright colors. In the same way that it changed colors, it oscillated back and forth between urchin-like and octopus-like in a matter of milliseconds. At first, its movement seemed smooth and flowing, like a super-fast snail, but upon further inspection, it reminded him of saccades, that rapid eye movement that looked smooth but was an aggregation of hundreds of super-fast, jerky fixations.

"Guys! It's behind me!" Tad was both jubilant it was out of him and horrified that it was slowly making its way back.

"Don't you fucking move!" they all screamed. The doctors only stared at him. Why didn't they say something? Help him explain what was happening?

Halfway up the bar, it did a thing. That thing was appearing in one spot for one second, and then suddenly appearing a few inches farther along its path in what appeared an instantaneous event. Tad screamed, "Heeeey!"

He'd been dropped off as a young teen at the skating rink and been skating when they put on the strobe light. When you danced around, your arms and legs were in one place and then magically in another. This thing was moving like that, but in full hospital lights. It did it again.

"Don't you fucking move, motherfucker!"

Tad's head swiveling back and forth from the thing crawling towards his naked butt and the doctors and the cops.

To the doctors, he screamed, "Tell them! Did you tell them?"

They said nothing. It strobed again. He butt shuffled forward with his ass cheeks so it wouldn't crawl onto him. It strobed over the edge and onto the table directly behind him.

"Jesus fucking Christ! Do you not see it!" Tad screamed.

"Don't you fucking mo—"

"I'm going to just step down on the floor," he said. "All I'm doing—"

The cops yelling, eyes widening. The doctors slowly shuffling toward the door. Tad trying to slide his ass off the edge of the table with his hands up. The thing behind him strobing to his lower back. Tad screaming. The cops screaming. Tad looking over and seeing that, yes, there was a silver bowl on the trolley next to him with some melted ice and one piece of shrimp left. The cops emptying their guns.

Mahogany

Is this how dogs and cats wake up? Tad thought. No grogginess or lingering dreams. As an evolutionary byproduct, you're asleep one second and fully awake the next. None of your limbs are asleep either. On one hand, he thought never hitting the snooze button again would be pretty amazing. On the other hand, he had an octo-urchin inside him.

Those super bright surgery room lights were gone. In fact, the surgery room was gone. Tad was leaning over on some pillows. And not dead. Yes, he was alive. Which made no sense because he could still feel the sharp, stinging pain that accompanied the feeling of getting hit with a multitude of baseball bats at the same time. Then hitting the floor. Then gasping for air that wouldn't come and looking over to his side to see the bloodied body of a doctor that had been prodding him. So why wasn't he dead?

But he already knew the answer. The same thing that was causing all of this calamity was probably the same thing that had saved him. What else? Tad sat upright and put a hand on his chest. He was dressed? In his clothes.

"This is a dream," he said aloud.

"No, but it is rather surreal," said a voice from the aether.

Tad took in his surroundings. He'd been in one of these as a teen, for prom. A limousine. This one was fancier somehow. The mahogany. The subtle lighting. Who knows what actually makes things fancy? Is it a certain type of wood?

"How are you feeling, Mr. Gruber?"

The voice was male, confident, leisurely. And there it was again, the Mister. Even in the mist of confusion and anxiety, that felt good. A tiny bit of respect for the man of the hour. The man who swallowed an anomaly at one point.

Tad asked, "What the hell happened? I should be dead."

"Well," said the slightly British-sounding voice, "I'm not certain anyone 'should' be dead, but one would certainly have expected you to be by this point. I believe your newly acquired friend may have helped you out in that respect."

Tad could think of nothing to say. So, he didn't. The voice was silent as well. Tad's sense of time was skewed. He had no idea how long he'd been out. Hours? Days? Tad's mind raced in all possible directions for a bit, then calmed. He was impatient, just sitting there. How long could this trip be? Why didn't he feel like he should escape? Who escapes mahogany? Tad made a note that if he ever kidnapped anyone, he would do so in a very fancy van to help along the Stockholm Syndrome. Had he been rescued?

He was tired of thinking and worrying and wanted all thought removed until he had answers. Then he thought about how easy it was to wake up so fully so quickly and had an idea. He thought about falling asleep. Maybe he could fall asleep as quickly as—

Another Warm Blanket

Tad awoke. The door to the limousine open and a very bright, outside sun blinding him. What else to do? He got out. He put his hands over his eyes to shield them and saw that he was surrounded. A semicircle of what appeared to be wait staff (is that what you call them?) was standing in front of him. A mix of men and women in different modes of dress. He supposed they each had a specialty.

"Hi," he said to everyone, sounding to himself like it was his first day in kindergarten.

An older gentleman in the middle of the arc stepped forward and offered the slightest bow.

"This way, sir," he said and began to walk toward the entrance of a house that was more of a castle. In fact, looking up, he saw a couple of stone turrets here and there. The house stretched for a way to his right, and looking to his left he saw that it went the same distance and then doglegged and carried on in that direction for a bit. He'd never seen a house long enough to dogleg. A hole on a golf course, yes, but a house? How many stories was this thing? As he stepped under the portico (is that what you call it? Yes, he was pretty sure that was the correct term and how did he, Tad, know that?) he counted at least four floors, although it was hard to tell because some of the architecture and window placements were a little off.

As he stood in the foyer, Tad watched the wait staff tote his belongings into this mansion. First, there were his suitcases, then the contents from his desk and closet. His board games. All his stuff. Okay. They expected him to stay here? To move in?

The old man said, "Mr. Cashmore will see you in the study," pointing the way, but not moving.

Tad marveled at his surroundings. It wasn't as gaudy as he suspected it would be, all white marble and gold trim, but every flourish and painting did let you know that money wasn't an issue. How tall is that one painting? Eight feet, maybe? He entered the study and saw a middle-aged white guy with a perfectly trimmed beard. He was smiling at Tad as if he were the man's long-lost son.

He sat opposite the man in a chair that had probably been constructed for that eight-foot-tall man in the painting. His feet barely touched the floor. He was about to return what he could of the smile, when he caught a whiff of the beach, or the sea, or the more it assaulted his nostrils, something dead washed ashore that had baked in the sun. He looked over to see a large, aluminum bucket sitting at the edge of the room.

"Eeegkkt." He gagged.

The man's smile unwavering. Then a movement in his nether regions and Tad's pants were full. Did he just shit himself full-service, sitting in this expensive chair? No, he realized. He did not. Because one's poop doesn't slither out of one's pants and move down the chair and across the floor with lightning speed. Tad didn't panic as he expected he probably should. He didn't even feel it coming out. How? Did it matter at this point? No. It was out. He stood up as it disappeared into the bucket.

"Eegkt!"

The man said, "Sorry for the smell. We'll fix that."

"Look, thanks for whatever you did," Tad pointing at the bucket, "and for getting that thing out of me. But I need to get the fuck out of here while it's out. I need to... to... go home."

That smile. That smile reeked of bemused curiosity. The man grabbed a remote and a TV came out of nowhere on the wall. He scanned through some news stations until he hit the right one. A man with a fifty-dollar haircut was donning a look of concern.

"In other news, our local hospital was on lockdown earlier today after a shooting left several doctors and police officers dead. The police haven't released any information but say they would like to talk to this man, Tad Gruber, in connection with the event. If you have any information or know of his whereabouts, please contact the police." Tad saw his picture pop up in the corner of the screen and then it was quickly replaced by someone frozen in midair, basketball inches from both hands.

"In other news, the Ridley Jayhawks have made it to state for the first time in a decade. In overtime—"

The TV went black and then disappeared back to its hiding place. He was wanted. For butthole murder. He turned to Cashmore, whose smile was unchanged.

"Are you keeping me prisoner?" Tad asked.

"I'm providing you a hideout. I'm technically aiding and abetting, correct?" the man said.

Tad shrugged, was about to try and answer, because that's what you did when someone asks you a question, when another voice from the aether did it for him.

"Correct, sir."

So many voices emanating from elsewhere. Must be his lawyer. Rich people had lawyers stashed everywhere. In their closets, basements, and under the wings of their private jets.

Tad thought for a moment. The water splashed out of the bucket and onto the fancy rug. Cashmore was unaffected. A realization pouring over Tad.

"You want it to stay in me?"

The man nodded ever so slightly.

"Why? It eats shrimp and poops out worms."

"Well, Mr. Gruber, it does more than that now, doesn't it?" Cashmore leaned over and brought out a fancy little transparent box of beveled glass. The box was no bigger than a Rubix Cube. In the middle, on a tiny dais, was Tad's book.

"That's mine," Tad found himself stating. Was it his? "Correct?" he projected to the aether.

"Correct, Mr. Gruber," the voice stated solemnly.

Cashmore set it in front of him on the coffee table. "Of course it's yours. Copyrighted through film and, of course, you're listed as the author. I've taken the liberty of having it professionally cleaned and sealed."

Tad said, "Well... Good. But why would... so, you want more tiny books? What good are... I don't understand."

The man smiled wider and said, "My boy, you have an alien or supernatural creature of some sort that has taken to you as a host. It has created, somehow, with your help, a tiny book, in full. This is an unheard-of occurrence. Rarity such as this is the penultimate of high art."

"You want me to have that thing stay inside of me so it can make you a library of very strange literature? I don't think so. That fucking thing is not going back inside me." Tad moved a couple of steps away from the splashing and toward the door.

Cashmore said, "I'd like to pay you ten million dollars per book. I've already deposited the first ten million for this book into your account, as a gesture of goodwill."

Tad stopped backing toward the door and pulled out his phone. He checked his bank app and stared at the number on the screen. $10,000,327. That was ten million more than he had at the start of his day. He looked at Mr. Cashmore.

"Per book?"

"Yes."

Tad looking at his phone. At the number. Per book. The thing sloshing out of the bucket. Strobing across the fancy Persian rug. Tad's emotions on a rollercoaster. Cashmore saying he'll make some calls and sort out the police. Tad realizing the thing was a little bigger now, but still not feeling it as it crawled back inside him. Tad tearing up for reasons he couldn't quite put together. Thinking he had to set some type of boundaries or exert some kind of agency.

Tad said to the aether, "I would like a warm blanket."

Imposter Syndrome

The old man led Tad to his room. There was a warm blanket folded at the foot of his bed. It felt as if it had just been taken from a dryer. It took a couple of weeks to get into the groove of the rich life. Two weeks is really all it takes for anyone to get used to anything.

At first, Tad ordered all sorts of dishes he saw on his ridiculously large TV screen. He had the finest cuts of steak. He had never been able to cut a steak with his fork. Pastrami and cabbage something, another that melted in the mouth. Carbonara and all manner of bacon. His favorite after two weeks of experimentation—Cajun bacon topped with sundried tomatoes and goat cheese.

After two weeks of wandering around the huge grounds and gardens, he asked the old man, who seemed to be the most attached to him, how he was to travel if he wanted. He was told to simply ask and they would provide. So, he asked to go to Paris. That evening, he was on a chopper, then a small private jet, then a much larger airplane that took him to France. Oddly enough, no one checked his passport, which was a good thing, because he didn't have one.

He stayed in a small villa on the outskirts of the city and came and went as he pleased. Spas, sightseeing, theatres, movies, and the best food at the best restaurants. He asked about other countries. He went to Belgium, Portugal, Germany, Italy, and Finland. He'd never felt so free. So good. So *Eddgkkt*.

That oversized shrimp flashing in his brain again. How could you crave something that made you gag?

Tad never received any calls on his phone except from his mom, whom he convinced that he'd taken a very cool job for a very rich man doing very cool stuff. None of which was really a lie. He paid off her house and put $20,000 into her bank account. He would have done more, but he thought it would draw too much attention. The police were no longer hot on his trail and when he read an article about his hometown massacre, it seemed to be that the police had shot someone hopped up on opioids. The news stations apologized for showing Tad's photo as he apparently had nothing to do with the incident. Still, it was an unspoken reality that keeping low to the ground was a good idea.

Tad's mindset was a bit more positive as well. He had turned that insecure vision of his former high school classmates on its head. In his new daydreams, he strides out onto the auditorium stage at his old school, all his old classmates staring expectantly up at him as he relates the story of how he became the richest man on Earth.

"And so you see, my fellow classmates, all you need is to be singled out as the perfect host by an alien organism. A host that provides the perfect biome in all of the universe to create the most sought after works of literature ever produced." Tad laughs. They laugh. "I know you are all thinking that's not possible. But with Mr. Gruber at your side, all things *are* possible. Look under your seats everyone!" he states knowingly. They do. There is screaming and panicking and strobing of ass urchins and people clenching their sphincters to no avail. Tad laughs maniacally and points, "You get an ass urchin, you get an ass urchin, everybody gets an ass urchin!"

"Mr. Gruber," says the voice.

Tad is smiling to himself. He looks up to see the old man.

"I believe it's time sir," the old, gray mustache states.

Even though Tad never seemed to have a clue, the old man appeared to always know when the next pot sticker was coming. That's what Tad called them now because the chrysalises did resemble semi-transparent, oil-slicked potstickers. This was his fifth book release. It was weird to think of poops as book releases, but that's what they were now. Indie poops.

"Time for a novel nugget?" he asked, laughing at his own joke.

"Sir," the old man says and holds his arm out in the direction of the bathroom. "They are ready."

Tad walks with confidence to the men's room. It's a rather upscale Parisian bistro and he and the old man weave through the tables and enter the bathroom. It's small, and only has one stall that is not working. No issue. Tad has a portable that was made specially for him. He pulls his pants to his knees and sits. There are two other men in the restroom. One is at the door and one is next to the old man, who is in front of him. He doesn't even feel it anymore and has to look down to make sure it's in there. He doesn't bother wiping either. He is always clean. Tad begins to stand up and for a moment he is exposed. This is when a man, who looks overdressed even for this Michelin-starred bistro, enters, glances at a young man with his dick out and three other men tending to him, and turns to exit. Tad laughs and thinks, you know, if I wanted, I *could* have three men service me in the bathroom.

This ignites a line of thinking that Tad has been turning over in his mind for a couple of weeks. He's incredibly horny and wants to get a woman, but doesn't want to catch anything or learn down the road he has offspring running around Europe. He's embarrassed but finally asks the old man, who states that this may happen organically in the next few weeks. That he needs to talk to Cashmore because there is a big surprise to unveil. Won't say what, though. Tad is dancing around the cobblestone streets like a drop of water in a hot pan. The Leidenfrost effect, he thinks. He can bring things like this to mind in a blink now. Before, he couldn't spell 'receive.'

Tad waited on pins and needles, swam in the outdoor pool, and worked out a little because he was getting soft and pudgy around the middle. And pale.

Yes, as Tad looked in various mirrors around town, he noticed he was... less than white. Off white? He had a doctor on call now. He would ask him later, on a private video.

After a couple hours, the old man answered his phone and shook his head as he hung up.

"What do we got this time?" Tad asked.

The old man said, "The title is *The Sleeping Princess*," Mr. Gruber. A particularly Baudelairian approach to an old witch's tale, related as a children's story, sir. A nice, stark juxtaposition. Nicely done."

"Thanks," Tad replied hesitantly, finally understanding the true meaning of imposter syndrome.

No More Country Music

Time passed. Tad grew even more comfortable with his newfound opulence. He visited his mom and bought her gifts. Not huge Maserati type gifts. His mom didn't want these things. She liked everything plain and simple. Her cars, her food, her life. He didn't rail against this, seeming to grasp on some level her repulsion at pomp and circumstance. Sometimes the more bells and whistles something had, the harder it was to deal with, especially when it ceased to function properly. He didn't fight back when she said that if he was going to buy her a new car, she wanted the windows to roll up by hand. He ordered the car and had it delivered. He cooked her butterbeans and cornbread with some onions on the side. Instead of moving into a nicer home, she stayed in the same house she'd lived in for the past forty-five years.

It was while he was visiting and lying in his old bed, drifting slowly towards a good night's sleep, that Tad realized he was comfortable. That is to say, the temperature in the room was perfect. It made sense because he had grown up in this room and so his body had probably come to accept this temperature as the best at which to fall asleep. This reminded him of his fancy, custom room at Cashmore's mansion. He never complained about it, because there was too much other cool stuff to play with, but the temp in his room seemed to fluctuate. One week it was a little hot. The next week, it was bordering on cold. It doesn't really matter when your comforter is temperature controlled. But now that he thought about it, the temp changes weren't confined to his room. They were that way in all parts of the house.

After a moment, this led him to think of the music. It was always playing in the background. Almost like a music score to a movie in that it was doing its job if you never recognized it. Doing its job, he thought. Yes, one week was country and the next pop and the next... something else. Almost... a pattern. He thought about other things and started to see patterns.

In his diet as well. Yes. Last week was very bread-heavy. It was subtle, but when you added it up, most meals were probably seventy percent bread. He thought backward, to places he'd been and meals he'd had. Before that, it was green vegetables, then meats, and then fruits. There were even patterns within patterns. Lamb for a few days, then goat, then duck. He had thought it the random cravings of a new-money, college graduate. But...

Tad called Cashmore. "Hey, Tad. What's up?"

Tad now, he thought. No more Mr. Gruber? Then chastised himself for having the thought. He was friendly with a billionaire. Of course, Cashmore could call him Tad. He thought about using Cashmore's first name in return.

"Hey, Mr. Cashmore," Tad said. "Um, are you experimenting on me?"

Cashmore always answered immediately, as if he had already had the conversation, and confidently, as if he was always in the right. This time, there was a slight hesitation.

"Yes." And then a silence that it was obvious he left for Tad to fill.

"Okay. In what ways?"

"Well, we are approaching this scientifically. I'm sure you've figured out the temperature fluctuations and changes to your diet, as well as the positioning protocol, correct?"

Protocol? Why did that word bother him so? Because it highlighted a specific aspect of a standard practice or procedure in cases such as scientific research and medical guidelines. That's why, he thought. And Tad had no idea what 'positioning' was.

"Of course," Tad said. He had learned to answer confidently from the best.

"We wanted to see if any of these environmental factors affected the product."

Product? There's yet another word to flag. Why? Because it symbolizes—

Cashmore said, "Look, your concerns about sex will be put to rest in a very favorable way on Saturday week. I've organized an auction."

It was Tuesday now. What the hell did Saturday week mean? He could never figure that out. Was that the Saturday after this Saturday? And another word to flag. Auction.

"Are you... selling me?" Tad asked. Cashmore laughed. Tad was certain he had never heard the man laugh before, and hearing it now was somehow startling.

"No, my boy. We're selling art. That fifty million in your account is about to jump quite a bit. We'll get you to nine figures soon enough."

Tad wrote nine zeros in chalk on his mental chalkboard. Then he changed the first zero to a one, then added comas. This was how his mind worked. One hundred million dollars. Even though that amount was only double what he had now, it seemed like so much more money. It was a whole other zero, mind you.

"I'll send you the schedule."

Tad said, "Wait, did it?"

"What is 'it'?"

"Did it change the—" Tad was going to say 'book', but then chose to match Cashmore's emotionally stark terminology, "product?"

"Well, all the stories are a little strange, but you could say that *The Sleeping Princess* was particularly unhinged. A good read, just the same. Overall, though, I would say no. You appear to stick to the horror genre. A niche genre, but then again, you have the most niche book in the entire world."

"Indeed," Tad said. Even when things got a little confrontational, Cashmore always de-escalated with ease and ended the conversation on something both parties agreed on. Tad was learning but doubted he could ever be this smooth all the time.

"Okay, thanks. And one more thing," Tad said. "No more country music. For the love of God, no more."

Cashmore laughed again. He was in quite a good mood.

"No problem, Tad. We'll start the contemporary Christian Wednesday next."

Sleep Gagnea

Tad was trying to read the schedule, but the news kept slipping into his ear. At some point, the algorithm had seen fit to show some "breaking" news before showing people failing and parking lot reviews. Some country attacking another country. Putin being a shithead again. Never-ending bullshit. He changed videos. Disc golf. That was peaceful enough. People throwing frisbees and hiking in the woods. Chill.

The schedule description was not chill. It was insane. He had called Cashmore three times since he read it. Each time feeling better by the end of the call, but then a panic building soon after. Before going to bed, he pulled off all his clothes and stood in front of the mirror. How much had he gained since being able to eat any dish he wanted at any time? There was no scale in the bathroom, so he asked the aether for one. He knew they were always listening. It didn't bother him anymore. In less than five minutes, he had a scale.

Two hundred and five pounds. The last time he was at a regular doctor, he was sure they said he was about one ninety. Fifteen pounds. In nine weeks. At this rate, they would be using a crane to extract him from his bedroom next summer. He pictured himself at six hundred pounds. He would slide across the Persian rug in his room until he reached the door, then proceeded to squeeze through it like an octopus through a quarter-sized hole. This was a crystal-clear image in his head, like he was looking through a View Master. Tad knew this came from his reverse cootchie critter. This no longer bothered him. Whatever it was, it made him a lot of money and kept mostly out of his head.

The one exception was the image of the oversized shrimp. Tad didn't understand why it would flash in his mind like it did. Maybe it was involuntary for the little shit scribbler, like it is for us when we get hungry and think about Swiss Rolls or pasta. At any point, he figured this image of him as an octoman was a weird attempt at comforting him. It seemed to be saying, look, look what we can do together. And could they? For a split second, Tad toured the grounds in his mind, searching for a small opening that he could try to fit through, then stopped himself abruptly. Perhaps some things should be left alone.

He would have to eat less and exercise more for the ten days leading up to the event. Maybe get out in the sun a little. He was so pale. Crawling under his absurdly soft covers, he panicked some more and fell asleep thinking of those dreams where you're in your underwear in class and you're so embarrassed and you can't fathom why you would be sitting here like this. During his sleep, about once every thirty minutes, Tad would gag to the point of almost throwing up. This did not affect his sleep.

Sunsets and Jello

Saturday next, they flew to an island and then took a very nice speed boat to another island. The boat deboarded after pulling into an actual cave on the side of a cliff. Tad was in a Bond movie. He was sure of it. He walked down a tunnel that had ocean water on both sides of a never-ending dock. He was sure there were sharks with lasers somewhere in that black water. The whole compound was the most extravagant thing he'd ever seen, dwarfing even Cashmore's mansion. His room had a balcony that sat above the waves, crashing into the rocks below. It was beautiful, but also smelled of the ocean. A nice smell to some, but to Tad it wreaked of dead clams. Why hadn't his little friend fixed his gag reflex?

He spent the next day alone in his room. He was waiting for whatever sex thing Cashmore had talked about to play out. He pictured some lady strolling in with three lines of the hottest chicks he'd ever seen. He would peruse all those naked bodies one by one, pretending to pick out only the highest quality chicks, then laugh and take them all. Thirty or more women all over his body. Lining them up and doing the dirty to each one for thirty seconds each, so he could get a taste of them all before giving out, which he would certainly do, early and often. How long would he last the first time? He pictured the game Operation. It would be like when you accidentally touched the metal. He would graze a thigh on the way in and *Eeeennnnggghhh*! Game over.

He got so excited that he thought about handling matters himself. That way, he could satisfy his current desires and last longer when it happened. But then he thought about the old man, constantly listening. Impossible. He also thought about his little author. Tad had no idea about the physiology of the human body, or how everything was connected down around the groin area. He pictured himself at the end, ready to bust a nut, and the octourchin shooting out the end of his dick. Nope. Just, nope.

At the end of the day, Tad watched the sunset over the ocean and was about to hit the sack when the old man came in with a covered dish. He hadn't asked for anything to eat, but the old man set it on the table just the same and removed the silver top. The red cube jiggled on the plate. About two inches square and transparent. The old man made to leave.

"Um, what's this?" Tad asked.

"Jello, sir."

"Yeah, and what's *in* the Jello?"

"Gelatin, sugar, some artificial colors and flavors."

"Aaaaaannnnd?"

"Yes, sir. A catalyst and some enzymes."

Tad looked at the Jello and then at the old man. Catalysts lower the activation energy needed for a chemical reaction to begin. Enzymes increase reaction rates.

"Are we doing new tests the night before the event?" Tad asked.

"I believe so, sir."

"Wouldn't that introduce variability and possibly derail an already proven process?"

"Perhaps, sir. Previous tests show remarkable improvements, however. The cost-benefit analyses have pointed in this direction, sir."

"Hmm."

Tad slurped his Jello that contained catalysts and enzymes, and watched as the last tip of a burnt orange flame as it was extinguished by the ocean.

Snails

The auction room was shaped like an egg. Avant-garde. The dome above was hard to make out without lights, but based on the curvature of the walls, it was maybe thirty feet high. Once in the room, Tad could find no imperfections or interruptions in the wall of the egg. Metallic. Smooth. A white tile sat on the floor in the middle of the room. It was ten feet by ten feet square and lit from underneath by a white light. This is where he would be displayed.

"Now?" Tad asked.

Cashmore said, "Not quite yet, my boy. You are the main attraction. We'll attend the others first and perhaps you won't feel so alone in the process."

"Others?"

Cashmore smiled and led the way. They entered another room designed just like the previous one. This one had a canvas, maybe three feet by four feet, sitting atop the square tile in the middle. There were already people in the room, spread out in a semicircle around the tile, speaking softly to each other.

After waiting a couple of minutes, a woman walked in through the door and proceeded to stand on the tile. With the rest of the room in darkness, and everyone else in shadows, the contrast was stark. She was very clearly on display.

She was a cute thing, maybe in her late twenties or early thirties. It was hard to tell. She was in shape, though, which Tad was not. He had only lost three pounds so far. She pulled off her robe and was naked underneath. With his pent-up expectations, Tad began to feel the blood rush to his groin and suddenly felt like he was in eighth grade again. Soon, they would call him to the chalkboard to work out a math problem in front of the class. He shifted himself in what he hoped was a natural-looking movement. It was a good thing they were at the back of the crowd.

People were shuffling around to get a better view. Moving closer. Tad had to move himself to get a line of sight. The woman turned around and squatted. A handler emerged from the shadows as quickly as a tennis ball boy and placed another white tile below her. Everyone held their breath. Then, after twenty seconds, they had to take a breath and do it again.

The first five minutes were intense with expectation. The next five minutes, less so. After fifteen minutes, people began to shuffle around and whisper. The woman looked nervously to her handler. Then, she put her hands on the floor in front of her. The muscles in her legs worked. Her muffled groans turned into a staccato of goat-like bleating. Did she howl for a second? The white tile turned red as droplets splashed onto it. Tad shifted back and forth, looked at Cashmore, who did not return his gaze as he was fixed on the woman.

Though it seemed like a lifetime, it must have been a couple of minutes before it slipped out and landed with a squishy flop on the tile. The ball boy ran over and removed the tile, taking it into a darkened edge of the egg where a light briefly illuminated a group of what looked like doctors as they worked to clean whatever this was. As they did so, they moved like actors on a sitcom, always preserving the open view to the audience, so they never lost sight of the thing on the tile. After five or so minutes of cleaning, they moved it to the canvas and somehow affixed the tile horizontally to the bottom of the white, stretched fabric. Other handlers came with towels and blotted her nether regions and helped her back into her robe. She limped away into the darkness and out the door.

Everyone crowded around the canvas, shoulders now touching, shuffling for position. Tad and Cashmore moved in as well. There on the tiny, white tile, was a chrysalis. Whatever was inside was pressing on the sides. Things were happening now. It must have taken it another full ten minutes before it pushed through far enough that the handler could help it escape from its potsticker. A few strokes of a rag to attend to the slimy residue, as if they were plating food, and it was by itself on the tile.

It was a snail.

A rather large snail, but a snail just the same. It moved, slowly, ever so slowly, towards the canvas. When it reached the canvas, it began sliming its way upward. Behind it, instead of a clear mucus, was an array of bright, almost neon colors. There was already detail in the tiny, wet swath it was leaving. Tad had the notion that maybe the image was already below a layer of something, and this snail was simply eating away the layer of paint that was over it. But no, the closer he looked, he could see the irregularities in the fabric. The snail was painting. It was painting a highly detailed, three-by-four painting.

Tad wondered for a second why the fact that there were others like him was kept secret. He would ask later, but of course, there would be a perfectly reasonable answer, and so then why even go down that road? He looked at the snail and then the size of the canvas. How? Then he remembered the Jello and how it helped with metabolic speed and Hulk-like transmogrification. He thought about the miniature books he and his friend normally created. Then he thought about a picture book. A big, thick, heavy coffee table book. Something that would wow the audience. How big would his anus author have to be to create something like that? And the blood. Was that normal? He thought of his bank account. He thought of his mom. Her, standing in the audience and watching while he squatted in front of a bunch of billionaires and pooped a pot sticker.

"Well, Tad. Really, son?" she says.

Field Goal

The ETA for completion of the painting was three and a half hours. Some people left quietly, as did Cashmore and Tad, Cashmore explaining that they could move between rooms as they pleased.

"How many others like me are here?" Tad asked.

"There are no others like you." A cryptic non-answer, powdered with flattery to block further questions.

"A snail that paints? C'mon. That's next level."

"Indeed. But the painting usually turns abstract after the first half, and she's only done miniatures to date, like yourself."

Tad's mind turned to the coffee table picture book again, sans the chrysalis step, turned sideways and stretching his ass like a breached newborn, screaming in pain while the affluent rattled their jewelry clapping. He died for his craft, they would say. A true artist, they would laud.

Cashmore finished, "And she can only do one a month. You're more productive by a factor of four. And your work... flawless. Yes, my boy, not a one like you."

Cashmore flashed his Cashmore smile as they entered the next room. Another female, young, on a tile already in her birthday suit. She squatted and bent forward on her hands so that her event horizon was visible to all. This was a quicker exit. Her muscles and flesh undulating and warping. Something inside coming out. Tad squinted. The crowd moved inward again to get a better look. At first, it looked like she was taking a chocolate, soft serve poo, but that wasn't quite right. It was rotating. Turning in circles as it came out.

As it touched the floor, it twisted and continued to rotate, wet and creamy, growing in size as she slowly, over a period of a couple of minutes, stood up from her spread-eagle squat. As Tad looked at the object, he suddenly realized what it was. Everyone's seen one, at least the finished version.

It was a vase.

The clay was wet and shiny. Once she pinched it off and it stopped turning, it held its form. The handlers moved in, taking her to the side and mopping her nether region and using some substance in spray bottles to coat the two-foot-tall creation. People clapping. An older man asking if he could touch it. No, he could not. Until after the auction. If he bought it. Cashmore relayed this information with his signature smile. A round of laughs from the audience.

In the next room, a man's chrysalis hatched what looked like the world's tiniest violin along with the bow. Tad thought of that saying, except it wasn't his heart bleeding for you, it was his ass. With each drop of blood that spilled onto those white tiles, Tad was growing more nervous. How much blood does the human body contain? How much can you lose and not die? And what if he did die? Would they keep him hooked up to machines that kept his body going so the most expensive book releases ever could keep going?

As they were leaving the room, they heard the melodic and warm notes behind them. Tad turned around to catch a glimpse of a tiny person with the violin under their chin. She was quite beautiful, and as he walked into the next egg-shaped room, he became certain that he had seen her in a horror movie series on some streaming service.

The man in the next room must have been over seven feet tall, his face long and gaunt. He didn't look unhealthy, just a huge man. When he squatted, his ass was probably still three feet off the ground. A tiny potsticker fell to the tile; tinier than the rest. An odd site considering the man's size. Then another. Then maybe fifty or so. There was a moment of anticipation, and then they all burst open like popcorn.

They were full of spiders.

They immediately scurried off into the shadows of the room. Someone, under whose feet they passed, shrieked. Some people closed in for a better look and a few backed up a couple of steps. Three or four more chrysalises hit the floor. More people backing up. Spiders erupting again, skittering in all directions. Then it was as if someone opened the floodgates. Tens and then hundreds of little potstickers falling to the floor. People screaming and running. One lady in a very elegant dress jumping onto the back of an unsuspecting man. Bumper cars, but with people. Cashmore stood perfectly still as people rushed by, so Tad did as well. When the man stood back up, there must have been a thousand or so spiders in the room and on the walls. They weren't huge, mind you, but they were still spiders.

Tad noticed the tall man scanning the enormous room with a look of satisfaction on his face.

"How many normally come out," Tad asked Cashmore.

"Three or four," he answered, smiling ear to ear as he too surveyed the man's handiwork.

As Tad watched, several of the spiders that were somewhere in the darkened space overhead began dropping from the ceiling. Since no one else was panicking, Tad decided not to either. Until some of the spiders that were midway down began to move toward each other, accompanied by a tinny sound that reverberated off the walls. They weaved their webs together and moved through the air at angles running against gravity. He closed his eyes and listened. Yes. That sound was the chittering drone of thousands of wings flapping at a high frequency. The entire room appeared to be flaking away, tiny spiders with wings taking to flight and headed toward the middle of the room. No matter where you were standing in the room, you were in their path. Everyone ducking, some crawling. No matter. You couldn't help but run into them. They scampered over the patrons, paying them no mind, and headed on their way, but since this wasn't entirely apparent, there were intermittent voices of, we'll say disapproval, that echoed throughout the egg. Even Cashmore seemed a little unsure of himself as he attempted to weave his way through the arachnid obstacle course.

In the short hallway between the spider room and the next, they met the old man. Tad was rubbing his hands all over his body and making sure nothing had gotten down the back of his shirt collar.

"Sir, it's time," he said, raising his hand in the direction of a hidden door to their right. The lights in the hallway dimmed and then brightened, changing colors to a dark purple. A sultry voice from the aether informing everyone to attend the main room.

Everyone around him walking faster. Getting undressed as soon as he entered a small, regular-shaped room. Putting on his robe. Wondering why all the robes were white when there was so much blood involved. Not having time to panic properly before they open the door and motion for him to take the stage.

Tad looked out at a much bigger audience in a much bigger room. A hundred? Maybe more? How many billionaires were there in the world? Tad turning around and squatting down. Bending his head to see that a ten-million-dollar pot sticker hit the tile. About to stand up when another hits. Then another. Waiting on pins and needles. Thinking about scale. Business people were always talking about scale. Picturing what happened to the spider guy happening to him. Thousands of gyoza pouring from his rump like a portal into the cold storage of an Asian restaurant. Feeling a light touch on the shoulder by the old man. A cue that it was over. Standing and putting on the robe. Looking down and seeing no blood. No handlers touching his product.

It didn't take fifteen or twenty minutes for the chrysalises to come out. Only seconds. They shuddered like Mexican jumping beans and then started to grow, bursting at the seams. They tripled in size. Then doubled. Where the extra flesh came from, he had no idea. Everyone crowded in. The dark walls of the egg lit up and large, rectangular swaths of wall turned from black to high-def video of the forms on the back-lit tile. They stretched in all directions simultaneously, while at the same time flattening. Then they caught on fire. He noticed the handlers did not move, but gave each other the side eye, as if to say, um, are we supposed to put that out?

The flames burned out as quickly as they had flamed up, and there was only the blackened, green crust in the shape of a flattened rectangular prism. A nod from Cashmore and the handlers moved forward. Again, that confidence when you really had no idea what you were doing. An extremely valuable tool to have in your belt.

The handlers took to the tile with tweezers and scalpels and all manner of cleaners and wipes. The crust cracked as they pulled it apart. The cleaning and then a nod to Tad from Cashmore in the direction of the door. It was apparently in bad taste for the artist to hang around when the product was the thing on display. And of course, it could take away some of the mystery. But Tad did not move. He had learned another very important lesson from hanging around rich people. Most of the time, you could do whatever the fuck you wanted, and nothing would come of it.

As the handlers finished and stepped back, Cashmore stepped forward and carefully picked up each book, inspecting the spine and then the title page. Then setting them down and standing to address the audience with the biggest smile he'd ever put on. It was a genuinely happy smile that included the eyes and all the other happy parts of his face.

"It's a series!" he announced.

Ten percent of the world's wealth clapped with excitement.

Tad stepped forward from the shadows to stand next to Cashmore and without even thinking about it dropped his robe completely and shot his arms up like he'd made a field goal. The crowd erupted and filled the giant egg with cheers and laughter.

Pimped Out

Tad sat on the plush, semi-circular sofa and stared out at the ocean's dim froth in the moonlight. He had never been so happy and confused at the same time. After what he'd been through, Tad had the notion that nothing could surprise him, but tonight did. Cashmore disappeared to prepare for the coming auction. The butt snail was only halfway through its painting. A series! He knew people liked series more than standalone novels. What would it go for? Could it bring fifty million? Surely it could. That was all well and good, but they had hinted at his sexual desires being fulfilled here at the auction site. Where was this line of women to pick from?

"Where's the women?" he asked the aether.

The old man entered the room two minutes later and put his arm out to indicate the direction Tad should travel in. Tad pulled his robe tight and made his way down the hall, slowing to let the old man pass because he had no idea where they were headed. They went down three sets of stairs, which Tad questioned, then figured the other guests were probably using the elevators. These hallways and rooms looked considerably less elegant, and he guessed these were the staff quarters, although they were empty. They came to a larger open room, maybe a gathering area, and Tad saw three women talking at a table, sipping mixed drinks. To their right was a large bed that was certainly not usually present in the room, a fireplace, sauna, and a very familiar, aluminum bucket next to the wall.

The old man bowed out and left Tad standing in front of the women. They were all decent-looking. They appraised him, smiling. As the blood began rushing to his nether regions, he noticed their dress and straightforward appearance. These weren't hookers, these were guests. These were billionaires.

"This your first time doing something like this?" one asked. The others laughed. "You sure you're okay being pimped out? Cashmore said you might be a little shy."

She had a sparkle in her eye but was feeling the situation out just the same. Tad didn't want it to appear like this was his first time. He moved forward and pulled his robe apart, his member already halfway there, but now frozen like an upside-down smile in space. He'd never been naked in front of more than one woman. Especially three. Especially billionaires.

"I'm going to drain you completely, love. I'm getting every penny's worth," another said.

Holy shit! He has pimped me out.

At this moment, though, Tad couldn't bring himself to be offended. He hardened the rest of the way as the first woman knelt from her sitting position and, looking into his eyes, took him in her mouth. The other two stood and began slipping out of their clothes. These were bodies that had personal trainers attached to them. Tad was still flabby in the middle.

He came almost immediately. He moaned. She moaned. He kissed them on the mouth. He took their hard nipples in his mouth, then they moved to the bed where he had them lie back with their feet pulled up. He explored each one with his tongue and then his still-hard cock. When things wound down and everyone had their fill, they all lay on the bed, staring at the ceiling.

Tad said, "That was the best thing that's ever happened to me." He meant it. They laughed. He laughed. Then the wilder one said, "I want to see it." She propped up on her elbows and gave Tad an expectant grin. How could he say no to that, after what they just did to him?

"Sure," he said, getting up and walking over to the bucket to verify there were shrimp in there. And, indeed, there were. In fact, these were live. No expense spared, he thought. Then he walked over to the bar and squatted down. As he did, the wild one jumped up and sprinted over to the bucket, grabbed a shrimp out, and ripped its head clean off. Tad did not see this. Nor, while he waited bent over, did he see her quickly peel it and lie spread eagle on the floor in the path from his ass to the bucket. Only when the other two OMGed in shock did he awkwardly bend his head around to see her shove a freshly peeled shrimp into her vagina.

"Oh, I don't think... I wouldn't—" he started, but it was already strobing across the tiles. "Oh, shit. Listen, I don't know if that's safe. I—"

Everyone watched as it strobed to within a few inches of her already dripping love hatch. Now that it was in front of her, morphing back and forth from an urchin-like thing with spines and an octopus-like thing with suction cups, her facial expressions belied a self-doubt that was growing by the minute. In fact, she had changed her mind completely and was about to get up when it entered her.

And for the first time, Tad saw how it slithered into the human body. He knew octopuses could squeeze through holes the size of a quarter, so Tad had always assumed that it squished itself into an impossibly small cylinder and slid in. This was not the case.

It didn't squish down at all. One minute, her vagina was the perfect size for a happy penis, and the next it looked like a reverse childbirth. It all happened so fast, there was no time to react, so she remained very still, sitting spread eagle in the middle of the room.

"Oh my god," she said, a permanent look of panic now engrained on her face. "How did I not feel that?" And then, "Oh, shit. It's moving around."

She looked down. Everyone looked down, staring at her shrimp-filled love purse. One full minute passed. Then another. This was the longest stretch of time that anyone in the universe had ever sat perfectly still and stared at a wet vagina without doing *something.* Then, with a look of concern that somehow surpassed panic, she put her hand to her stomach, then slowly raised it to her chest. She looked up at Tad with an expression he would later think of as a rather sad resignation, then her head exploded.

Eyeless Sockets

Where the woman's head used to be was his author friend. Its urchin spines and tentacles were all extended in a manner that hinted it might have stuck its tentacles in a light socket. As if someone had put a firecracker inside it which then exploded, taking her head with it. Her head was everywhere, or rather, tiny, tiny little pieces of her brain and scalp and skull were everywhere. By everywhere, I mean in an evenly distributed spherical pattern from right next to her on the tiles to the far corners of the room. This included Tad's mouth, which had been opened due to his slack-jawed appraisal of the situation just seconds before.

He threw up at his feet.

The other two women closed their legs rather suddenly and screamed. They jumped from the bed and ran for the door, slip-sliding in the thin layer of crimson covering the tiles.

Tad threw up again at his feet.

The old man walked into the room with a few towels as the women were running out. He did this calmly, as if this sort of thing happened all the time. The lights in the hallway turned red and began flashing or rotating, Tad couldn't tell which. The old man began wiping at Tad's face.

"Are you okay, sir?" he asked.

Tad threw up at his feet.

"I see, sir."

Tad looked up at his ass-mate as it seemed to relax from its overtly rigid state, letting its tentacles flow over the woman's shoulders. That's when he saw its face. *Wait, that can't be a face.* We're trained to see faces as a pattern from childhood. *This must be a trick of the light, or... I mean, it has no eyes if it...* and that's when the eyeless sockets blinked.

"What the fuck!" Tad screamed and turned and ran down the hall himself, naked and blood-sprayed, bathed in the red lights that pulsed on the walls of the corridor.

No Hard Feelings

Tad awoke. One minute there was no Tad and no room and no universe or anything, and the next moment he was wide awake. This is how he knew his little friend was back inside him. He sat up in bed, the same one he had just fled from because it was covered in blood and brains. He looked at his sheets and ceiling and floor tiles and was certain he was lucid dreaming that he was in a Tide commercial. Everything was clean and white.

It was daylight, so he knew some time had passed.

"How long have I been out?" he asked the aether.

"Fourteen hours, sir," came the answer.

"How..."

"We tranqed you, sir," the mild voice relayed.

"Ah," Tad said. Yes, he was in quite the panic. Had it coming, he supposed. The woman. *Oh my god, the woman.*

"That poor woman. How will... I mean... her family, and—" Tad stuttered.

"To your left, sir," the old man said.

Tad turned and saw the woman sitting on the couch. The thing was still on her head, which didn't make sense. It began to undulate, and the hollowed-out gullet began to make sounds that sounded like a toilet plunger being worked quickly, rubber being ripped apart, and mouse traps all at the same time. When she was done, the old man's voice entered the room again.

"She says no hard feelings. That it's quite exhilarating and the most exotic transition she's ever been through. Says she swam in the lagoon for hours this morning. She will have to change communication protocols, but all in all, she'll get along. Would like to know if you're okay."

"Yes. Fine, thank you."

Cashmore burst through the doors like a madman. His eyes were wild, feral.

"My boy!" he screamed at Tad, "You. Are. The fucking man! Do you know how much money is in your account now? I'll tell you. Thirty billion! What do you think about that, my boy!"

Tad tried to draw the zeros on the chalkboard in his mind, but there were too many.

"Yes. Fine, thank you," Tad said.

Camouflage and Rorschach

I said earlier that most people can get used to anything in a couple of weeks. Well, the latest developments were taking Tad a little longer to get past. Turns out the reason it goes into your butt is because if it comes in contact with your reproductive organs, it tends to reproduce itself in a rather violent and immediate manner. And although they used AI to communicate with octo-chick, he couldn't get her exploding head out of *his* head. And his companion had been strobing around for months all over the place. And his ass is only a few inches from his wanger. What if it just ducked in there for some fucked up reason and BOOM! octo-dude for life. This led to sleepless nights and paranoid days. In fact, not that Cashmore noticed or said anything about it, but he hadn't written a book in over a month. Before, it was once a week, almost like clockwork. Was something wrong with it? By association, was something wrong with him? Did his anus author have writer's block?

He stayed inside for two months. His boredom then overpowered his paranoia, and he decided to go out and eat at a nice restaurant, in Belgium. He took a plane to Brussels airport and then checked into a five-star resort. At least the architecture was five stars. The service, not so much. This happened even at the most expensive hotels, so he didn't fret. But when the waiter brought him the wrong order of three huge shrimp surrounded by an abstract plating pattern that looked eerily familiar, he balked. Not one to usually voice loud complaints like some of the old money, Tad decided this would be his first scene in a restaurant. He turned from his plate to the waiter and was about to chastise him lightly when he noticed that the waiter was standing wide-eyed, unmoving. Tad looked around; the whites of people's eyes began popping up all over the room. Silence engulfed the room.

At first, he thought he was on some kind of Truman show. They had hired all these people to attend the restaurant to make him feel at home. And when the waiter screwed up his order, everyone was just as taken aback as he was. But no, because a few people were taking out their phones and trying to discreetly take his picture. Tad felt a tug on his arm. The old man squeezing in between him and the waiter and the other two men that always appeared from nowhere were surrounding him, leading him from his seat.

Walking down the short hallway to the foyer, Tad put his hands to his head and made sure there weren't any tentacles where his hair used to be. He seemed fine. So, what in the hell was all this about?

As he passed through the foyer, he looked in the mirror and saw his face and neck. He was changing colors. Bright as a neon sign. So many colors, so fast. He was camouflaging.

Tad tried to compose himself as he made the tiny walk from the door to the waiting car, but when a dog barked somewhere to his left, he squirted ink so hard it tore through his pants and painted a Rorschach on the concrete behind him. He jumped into the back seat of the car.

This can't possibly get any worse, he thought, catching part of the news on the radio that the driver turned off when he hopped into the car.

"The U.S. has declared war on Canada."

Free Time

Tad stared out of the cave at the blue sky, bluer water, and puffy white clouds. He closed his eyes and imagined each of his chakras, slowly, and in turn. He could do this now.

Slow down.

Take a minute.

At first, he had no idea how to relax or meditate, or even what a chakra was. Well, he still didn't know what a chakra was, but he did know what color he imagined them to be, and how they were shaped like tiny suns, and that they helped you focus on certain parts of your body. And if you were focusing on your body and In the Now, then you didn't think about the past two months in the real world.

Things you can do with billions of dollars:

1) Pay cash for a boat on one of your excursions to Sicily

2) Pay cash for a small island an hour away from where you bought the boat

3) Hide out on said island for two months with an existing staff that was happy to have their salaries tripled. Money buys silence as well as happiness

After pretending to relax for a few weeks in a manner consistent with how you've seen other people relax, you have a moment of self-realization that you are, in fact, relaxing.

Never mind the fact that when the tide rolled in, the cave flooded. When you have fifteen dedicated souls at your discretion, you can decorate your temporary meditation cave the same as you would a room in your thirty-seven-room mansion. They come move it all out before high tide, then put it all back at low tide. Every day.

Tad had become used to people running around, catering to his every wish. But this seemed oppressively redundant, even to him. Like those old military stories where they make the Privates dig holes just to fill said holes.

But the camouflaging had slowly come to a halt. Maybe he would soon be able to go out in public. He smiled at the thought. *Thought.* That was another luxury he had. Tad never realized how much of a valuable resource time was. Normal people don't have time to think. They were too busy working to pay bills. As Yoda might say, "There is no think, only do."

Most people roll out of bed into the already spinning hamster wheel of chaos and ritual. If the boss catches you standing there *thinking,* they're going to ask you why the hell you're not *doing.* Thinking requires time. Free time. Who the fuck has free time?

In the Moment

As Tad finished visualizing his groin chakra, he became aware of a need, though for what he couldn't say. Perhaps getting in touch with your body accounts for strange feelings. But this vague compulsion was familiar. Then it hit him, softly, because he was chill, but hit him just the same. If the old man were around, he would be holding out his arm towards the portable potty. How he knew was still beyond him. Maybe it was in the job description. *Must be between the ages of 60 and 80, but move like you're 40, and must be able to tell when other people have to poop.* Had there been a tell this whole time? Had his earlobes changed colors when he had to poop a magic potsticker?

Proud of himself for being so in the moment, he walked over to the edge of the cave where the potty was and squatted, felt something emerge, then turned around without wiping to see what he had produced. The chrysalis's existence was a given. Always the same chrysalis with the same watery oil-slick rainbow of colors. But the time it took for the books to emerge, at least back at the rich folk egg-pods, had shrunk down to seconds, and this was the case now.

Existential Dread

Suffocating.

Mouth closed and you can't open it because you're underwater or under something. Arms flailing because that's what you do when you're drowning. A hand catching an irregularity, ripping, tearing, air running out. A light. An opening in the mire. Gasping for breath. Finally sucking in air before you were about to pass out. Wiping gunk from your eyes. Something sticking to all parts of your body. Peeling it off and taking a second to get your bearings.

You were just pooping or publishing, not sure which, and then you were drowning. Now you're sitting down and finally catching your breath. Everything around you is huge. Wait... no. No, it's not. You're small. And a much larger version of you is staring down at you.

"What the fuck?" you say. "What happened?"

You want to catch your bearings.

Bigger you says, "I just pooped you."

You realize you will never catch your bearings.

"Yeah, I'm having trouble processing this. I'm going to need a minute."

Bigger you says, "Okay. Me too."

A general sense of foreboding and existential dread breaks on the shore of your fragile mind. You are in an enormous cave with a Godzilla-sized doppelgänger. You know you are you but don't feel complete, like someone has pulled a Jenga piece from your essence and now there's a gap somewhere. You don't know what this hollow place is, but you are keenly aware that it was part of a foundation that kept your entire being from crumbling to the ground. How did you shrink down to the size you are now? What happened that—

Then it hits you. You *are* you. And you are bigger you. You are both. The bigger you, and you know this because you can remember this, squatted to lay his next publication, and then nothing. *You* emerge from the chrysalis. You don't remember getting up from dry pooping because you never did. Bigger you got up while you fought for air. You have all of bigger you's memories up to the point you came into existence. This is when you remember something from a childhood playground and laugh.

"What?" the voice booms above you.

Looking up, you say, "A silly joke from when I... we were kids. Very fitting now, I suppose."

The other you is searching in the dark, so you give him the first part.

"Have you ever had pussy lips stretched over your head?" you ask.

Bigger you smirks, and says, "No."

You say, "Then I guess you were an ass baby."

You both force a clipped laugh.

Big you asks, "Um... you need to wash off or something?"

Hermit Crabs

Small Tad says something.

"What?" said Tad. The other him was very small; maybe three inches tall. Which meant the sounds coming out of his mouth were smaller. And the ocean was oceaning and the wind was winding. The small voice relayed an ass joke from their youth, which both seemed to appreciate. Then they talked for a few minutes about how tiny Tad must have come to be.

"Okay, so we understand what happened," big Tad said. "But why?"

"Introspection. I'm a metaphor IRL."

Tad had no idea what this meant, so he looked away for a second, then looked back. This is the international sign for *I don't understand what you mean.*

"I mean talking to yourself about yourself. Trying to get a handle on life."

Tad had scooped some ocean water into a bucket and put one press of foamy soap in it. They talked while tiny Tad bathed in the water, Tad turning his head so as not to stare at his own nakedness, which made absolutely no sense, but he felt less creepy not seeing his own tiny penis. For the first time in his life, Tad felt as if his penis was huge.

"So, we can't be self-aware?" Tad said, more to himself than anything.

"I think lingering on things, for us anyway, can trickle down to our parasites as some set of instructions. You want to start writing? They write books. You want to look inward. They focus on that. They're like if our subconscious had an action plan."

As they talked, Tad noticed something about tiny Tad that was off. He couldn't tell what. Tiny Tad also noticed this but couldn't put his finger on it either. Tad retrieved tiny Tad's clothes from the rocks where they were drying in the sun and tiny Tad dressed himself on the table.

"Eating will be an issue. Not getting attacked by seagulls will be an issue. People ratting me out for a buck will be an issue. Communication without yelling until I'm hoarse will be an issue. And medically? Jesus Christ. If anything goes wrong, I'm totally fucked."

Tad realized after listening to tiny Tad talk for a few minutes what was off. There was a pervasive sadness emanating from him. Tad wondered if he himself felt this way. Should he? Of course, tiny Tad felt this way because he was small. Everything is more difficult if you are small. And there was no fix for this as far as he knew. Tiny Tad would have to live the rest of his life like this. Never-ending, chronic smallness.

Tiny Tad sat on the table and crossed his legs. Big Tad sat in the chair and stared at himself. He looked for imperfections or weird anomalies but found none. It was him. Just smaller.

"I don't mean to be rude," said tiny Tad, "but I'm going to need some time to think through things. We've gotta figure some things out pretty quickly."

Tad shuffled in his seat and tried to think of things that would need thinking through. But the only thing he could think of was that he just shat himself. Literally. And then, as if Cashmore had infected his brain, he wondered how much tiny Tad would bring at an auction. This was the world's first shrunken person. This was a harsh way to think about another Tad. He wondered if these thoughts had crossed Cashmore's mind. How to best market big Tad. Never mind fixing or saving him. What's your ROI? Tad looked over at tiny Tad and had another thought.

When he was little, he wanted a hermit crab he'd seen in a mall store. There was an argument with his parents that Tad somehow won, and he went home with two hermit crabs. Within three weeks, they were both dead. It took another couple of weeks to figure this out because, well, they were hermit crabs. When Tad was questioned about how much he was feeding them, he looked confused. Then he started to cry. This is a process young Tad would grow to repeat over the years due to his aloof nature and lack of interest in, well, everything. He was not curious about anything. Ever. So, when his dad calmed him by explaining that the hermit crabs had probably gone on a hunger strike, Tad accepted this answer without question.

In his adolescent years, in a rare moment of reflection, he brought back this memory only to realize that he should never be responsible for a pet. Or rather, anything smaller than himself that relied on him to feed it. For a brief moment that he was later ashamed of, he wondered if it was best to bury tiny Tad in the sandy floor and let the tide come in.

As he drifted from his thoughts, he noticed tiny Tad watching him with a smirk on his face.

"Thinking about burying me in the sand and forgetting about all this?" tiny Tad asked.

"What? No!" he answered, a bit too emphatically. "I was just thinking of what needed to be worked out, same as you?"

"So, what did you come up with?"

Tiny Tad knew he had nothing, which meant that tiny Tad was kind of being a dick. Maybe he would bury him. Tiny Tad smiled wide.

"Now you're definitely thinking about burying me. You couldn't live with yourself. We both know this."

Tad shuffled in his chair. He said, "Wasn't a serious thought. I'm sure you've..." Tad trailed off. He had no idea what tiny Tad was thinking.

"Look, I have all of your memories up to the point you pooped me out. Makes sense, I guess, to have that gap there. I was squeezing myself out, wow this is so meta, and then nothing until I scraped through the placenta." Tad had never thought of that boogery outer layer as a placenta. Was it a placenta?

"And so, there's the day-to-day; communication, feeding, safety hazards due to my size, possible leaks from the staff if I'm seen, transportation, delivery of information. I mean, you can barely hear me. We need a way for me to not have to scream every conversation. How to cut up my food. What best to eat for tiny organs to digest. What's my life... expectancy? And so on."

Tad said, "Okay."

Tad and tiny Tad turned to the cave's front arch. They could both hear the faint, faraway thumping of helicopter blades.

"They found us," they both said at the same time. And when it was close enough to see details, they said, "Okay, that looks military."

Tad walked towards the beach and tiny Tad started yelling, "Hey, hey, hey!"

"What? I'll see what they want," Tad said.

"Hey, man. They can't know about me. No offense, but I'm not going on an auction block. Look, I trust the chef. Call him and tell him to come down by himself with a bucket. I'll handle the rest. The tide is coming in shortly."

Tad protested, though for what reason he couldn't say.

"Why can't you just communicate with me?"

"Because they're probably coming to collect you. Military helicopters don't show up to sit and have tea."

Egg on the Floor

Tad ducked his head and got in the helicopter. He did this for two reasons. One, the old man had hopped down and extended his arm toward the door, and though he hated to admit it, he was like Pavlov's dog when the old man did this. Two, it was a military-looking helicopter and there was something in the back of his head telling him that if a military helicopter flew in to collect you, you were going to get collected, so you might as well do it on your terms and not let everyone see you getting dragged into it while you were flailing and screaming.

The only other occupants were two pilots and the old man. He watched the ocean for twenty minutes and then the city below for another thirty. He wondered if tiny Tad was doing okay. He'd made the call and explained what he could to the one person he trusted. His cook was a squat German expat who seemed like he'd always just received news he'd won the lottery. It was uplifting to be around people like that, but also a bit draining if he was being honest. How could anyone be that happy all the time?

The helicopter landed at an airfield and Tad followed the old man across the tarmac for a half mile, all the while thinking, "Hey, we're billionaires. Can't we use a golf cart or something?"

They came to a small, broken-down building with metal siding. It looked like a deserted gas station. They walked through a doorway with no door and past several rows of chip bags and candies from the 1950s. There was a layer of dust on everything that was so thick you almost couldn't make out the brands. In the back of the store, they stood in front of what looked to be a door to a freezer. It opened by sliding to the left, which was weird, until Tad stepped into the chamber and saw the elevator buttons. The old man placed his hand on a glass sensor and then pressed the blue button.

Tad's feet left the ground. Not by much, probably only a centimeter or so, but enough to give the impression of a free fall. His stomach clenched, as did his ass. The old man didn't seem to notice the elevator was reaching terminal velocity. After only a few seconds, the elevator came to a stop as abruptly as it had started. Tad thought, if there was a chicken in here, there would be an egg on the floor.

He followed the old man down a corridor and into an open area. Standing on a walkway and talking to some guy in a black suit was Cashmore. The man in the suit saw them and nodded, then walked away. Cashmore turned to them and walked over. The anxiety Tad was experiencing increased tenfold. It was Cashmore's face.

He wasn't smiling.

You First

"Tad," he said, almost formally.

"Yeah?"

"The Allied forces have asked for our help. Specifically, they believe you could be a huge advantage in the war."

"War?"

"You have been away for a bit," Cashmore said, walking across the boardwalk towards a door on the other side. Tad thought about not following and instead, very quietly turning around and tiptoeing through the door and then running down the hall back to the elevator. He did not for the same reason he got on the helicopter. He was already half a mile underground. He wasn't going anywhere. "Things escalated in the Middle East. Terrorist attacks all over Europe. China invaded Taiwan, Russia invaded Poland, which honestly was the last straw, but then they just marched right over to Alaska and bombed an airfield."

"So... is this... are we in..."

"World War III? Yes. So far, it's conventional. But the nuclear option is hanging over everyone's head. That's where you come in."

Tad thought of his mom. "Is my mom—"

Cashmore cut him off. "She's in Greenland. Underground bunker. Food and protection for years."

They walked through the door and into a room full of military officers. Conversations ceased when Tad and Cashmore walked into the room. One of the older, fatter men stood and walked over, extending his hand.

"Nice to meet you, son. I wish we had time for pleasantries, but let's save that for later. We've been briefed and seen the videos, as well as talked to the lady with the... uh... octopus head? Look, we need to see this thing you're in symbiosis with."

A *thunk* behind him. Tad turned to see a familiar bucket on the floor.

He said, "Sir, what exactly do you need me to do?"

The man with stars on his shoulders raised his bushy eyebrows and said, "Well, son, for starters, you can drop your drawers."

"You first," Tad said. He had no idea why he said it. Perhaps he was flustered and felt slightly threatened. But he intuitively knew not to talk like that to a man with that many stars on his uniform.

The general stared at him for a moment (generals are like Tom Cruise, good at staring intensely). Cashmore rubbed his hands together like he was about to join the conversation for de-escalation purposes when the general smirked a little and undid his pants, letting them fall to the floor, then grabbed his boxers and shoved them to the floor as well. He stood unabashed before the room. Tad couldn't help but look down and suddenly wished he was back watching tiny Tad bathing. Now he was even more insecure. The general wasn't ashamed because he had nothing to be ashamed of. In fact, thought Tad, if mine was that big I would walk around with it hanging out everywhere I went.

His bluff called, Tad pulled his pants down a little and bent over. His passenger exited and strobed over to the bucket, disappearing inside it with a splash. Tad stayed bent over so it could crawl back in, which it would do within the minute. The problem was that Tad's head was the same height as the general's crotch.

He tried not to look at the general's massive schlong while he waited for something to crawl back inside his asshole. He pictured his mom standing there and shaking her head back and forth disapprovingly.

"My lord, Tad!"

Glass Box

The general, transfixed, moved to get a better look. He did this by shuffling his feet in his downed trousers a few steps toward Tad, then to his side. Tad was sure he was closing the distance with his pants down on purpose. If there was someone in charge of measuring distances between massive penises and people's faces, they would have looked up and shouted to their apprentice taking notes, "Three feet and closing!"

Tad heard a splash and looked back to see his partner headed his way. As it nestled into his cubby hole, he remembered how the octo-lady's vagina had spread open to the size of a watermelon.

"Son," said the dazed general with genuine concern in his voice, turning directly toward him now, "Did that hurt at all?"

The man shouting to his apprentice, "Two and a half feet and directly addressing!"

Standing up, Tad said, "I don't feel anything when it happens."

He had never had another man's penis so close to him. Had it elongated slightly? He was sure if the general turned suddenly and then back again, it would slap him in the belly. Tad made a mental note to, in the future, always pull his pants down immediately if directed to by someone in the military.

The general held out his hands like he was showing how big the fish he caught was and said, "But you know that it... it's like this big and... I mean, it... expands your... "

"Yes, sir." Tad shrugged.

The general appeared to remember for the first time that his pants were down and pulled them up.

"I still don't understand what—"

"Look, son, the shit's hit the fan. We need you, like many men before you, to sacrifice your time and body for the sake of, well, not just your country at this point, but for the entire world. We've got your room ready."

Tad looked at Cashmore who gave him a poker face.

"Why do I get the feeling that I have no choice in the matter?"

The general said, "Because you don't."

Tad was beginning to think that maybe kicking and screaming was on the table after all. He thought of his alien, butt parasite and remembered that when threatened, it could definitely take care of business.

They left the room and began walking through a very long corridor. Tad turned to Cashmore who was unusually silent and expressionless. No smiles today.

Tad asked, "How exactly did you know to pick me up from the hospital?"

Cashmore glanced at the general, who gave a subtle nod, then said, "In early 2015, our world was invaded."

"Invaded? You mean like outer space invaded?" Tad asked.

"Outer space. Interdimensional. We're not really sure. The initial parasites selected easily manipulated hosts. I'm sure you've noticed a significant uptick in politicians and some of my billionaire friends that seem disconnected from reality? Chaos was the first order of business to shake our foundations. Then they held job fairs a few months ago all over the world. When you attended, I'm guessing you noticed the food was decidedly better than the usual fare?"

"Oh, man. It was. I had the best steak tacos I've ever eaten. And the salsa, so chunky, and with chips that held up while scooping. Oh shit. It was in the food. That was how they did it? A culinary invasion with the lure of job prospects in an economic downturn?"

"You've been watched closely ever since. We directed the doctors to attempt extraction during surgery."

Tad said, "The shrimp... to lure it out."

Cashmore said, "The pill-shaped camera you swallowed gave my friends at the Planetary Protection Office a good idea of what we're working with in your case. They're all invasive, but some are less symbiotic than yours. You're very lucky, my boy."

"But I produce books. What good are—"

"And here we are!" the general interrupted a little too loudly.

One of the soldiers opened the door to a room that was not shaped like an egg. In fact, the concrete and glass were put together in what Tad thought was possibly the ugliest manner possible. He wondered if this was what being worldly meant. The ability to give feedback on ugly architecture. It was the government, though. They were literally in charge of ugly architecture.

And the lighting. What the hell was up with the lighting? One corner of the room was dark. There was a light out overhead and the space was blocked by a stairwell that led up to a closet-sized glass box that rested halfway in the middle of a grated walkway. The furniture was stark, contemporary, with sharp angles. The plain, gray concrete looked smooth, like the tiniest bit of water would send you flying like a cartoon character stepping on a banana. There were no rails on the stairs. Were they trying to kill him?

Tad turned to ask them this very question only to see the door closing. Any ideas he had about retaining any agency at all disappeared when he saw there was no handle on the inside of the door.

"Well, then," he spoke to the aether. "I haven't eaten. When's dinner?"

Something pinged in the glass box above him and a frozen video appeared on the glass wall. He made his way up the stairs, carefully, since they were narrow as well as missing rails, and found himself standing in front of the glass box. There was no door, so he stepped forward and the video started playing. It was a video of a small girl lying on the ground at the foot of a building. Someone in an apartment complex was filming her from above. There was noise in the background. The video didn't have a lot of sound, but someone seemed to have turned the volume up to ten. Above the video, a numeric counter popped up in the form of an oversized, red LED. It had started at two hours and was counting down. The seconds ticked off.

The video panned and you could see two old women digging a trench in the yard. Then the camera panned back to the girl toddler who was lying on the ground. Tad's stomach clenched. He could see the rubble next to the building. Backing away from the glass box he stood again on the walkway. The screen and timer disappeared.

He jogged down the stairs and looked for other doors to other rooms. There were none. No bathroom. No kitchen. There was nothing. There was the room he was in and that was it. A sofa and a chair and one table.

"Restroom?" he screamed.

Ping!

Above him, the video appeared on the glass box wall.

Asshole Golfer

Tad sat on the sofa for a long while. He wasn't sure how long because he had put his phone in a basket when they arrived and never got it back. There were no clocks in the room, so unmeasured time passed even slower. He was incredibly hungry. It was especially difficult considering he usually got whatever food he wanted whenever he wanted it. His bladder was about to explode. Pooping was a thing of the past since his ass author moved in, and there was something to be said for never having to wipe, ever.

But he still peed like everyone else. And it had been a while. It felt like a thousand Lilliputians shiving him in the lower abdomen. He finally went over to the single circular grate on the floor that was in the darkened corner, unzipped his pants, and pissed as close to the grate as he could. Some went in and some splattered all around. Never mind. That's the way they wanted to play. Fine.

He sat and waited. The urine smell settled in the room like a miasma from a swamp surrounding a sewage treatment plant. Tad usually went with the flow, but it was impossible to ignore such a horrible smell.

"I'm not watching that shit!" he screamed to the aether. "Fuck you. Try some other experiment. This is ridiculous."

A loud sound shuddered across the room. Someone dragging a metal chair across tiles. Again, with the volume. It was incredibly jarring. At the end of the grated walkway, somewhere above him, a door slid open. One minute it was a wall and the next it was open.

A man strode through the door with purpose. The first thing you noticed was his build. He was lean and muscular, with cheekbones that meant something. He came down the stairs quick enough to make Tad stand up. He wore bright white pants and a pink golf shirt. He was tan. He looked like a Ronin or a Tanner. He walked up to Tad, who was taking stock of the situation, and punched him in the face before he could get a word out.

Tad's last fight had been in middle school. With a girl. When you get punched, you have to decide how to respond. If you decide to hit back, there's always the chance of the other person hitting you even more. But if you don't, they might decide to hit you anyway since you're not one for hitting back. So either way, Tad figured he might as well hit back. But these thoughts were late to the party, because the lean, asshole golfer had already turned and was halfway up the stairs.

He almost yelled *asshole* then thought better of it. His hand was covered in blood from holding his nose and his eyes were tearing up involuntarily. He had never been in the school of Real Men Don't Cry, but just the same, crying while in a fight doesn't generally build confidence. His nose was sting-throbbing. It had been a simple, straight punch, but goddamn! How could someone hit that hard without a roundhouse? He got up and walked around for several minutes, cursing under his breath. The bleeding eventually stopped, but there were no paper towels to wipe with, so over the next hour the blood coagulated all over his face. A couple of hours later, Tad came to a realization.

He was going to have to watch that horrible shit in the glass box if he wanted anything to eat. And he was starving. And if he started mouthing off, someone would come out and punch him in the face. In fact, he was a quarter mile underground in a military bunker, so they could do much worse if they liked. He steamed long enough to satisfy his ego and then walked up the stairs to the box, steeled himself, and walked forward into the transparent box.

The video popped up on the glass and the timer began its countdown. He watched as much as he could, then saw a loophole. Keeping his head facing straight, Tad averted his eyes by staring a few inches to the right of the video and focusing on the wall opposite. In a few seconds, there was a *Ping!* and the video and timer flashed off and on again. The video starting from the beginning as well as the timer.

"Oh, for fuck's sake."

He watched the video. And the next one. And the next one. He hadn't been on social media in months but remembered some of these clips. Others were new to him. Not all were bad. But that's how the algorithm plays with you. A giggle. A laugh. Some indifference. Then a girl of nine or ten carrying her smaller sister miles down a war-torn highway because she got hit by a car. And your brain tells you to turn this shit off and move on, but before you make the conscious decision to do so, your thumb scrolls without your consent from muscle memory and Jenna Ortega and Aubrey Plaza are standing next to each other at a podium and you can't look away and then fifteen minutes later you see something else that makes you hate humanity.

Tad glanced at the timer. 47 minutes 13 seconds. His stomach growled. He had lived such a life of pleasure and freedom for the last months that this was fucking with his reality. The unfairness of it. He understood what they were doing, but this was bullshit. As if they were reading his mind, on the opposite wall a huge map appeared. On the map, several Middle Eastern countries were colored in red. He didn't know their names, but some of the surrounding ones he did know. France and Spain were red. All of Russia and China were red. The northern parts of Africa, all red. A few smaller countries in South America were red. And for some reason, in the U.S., Florida and Texas were red. As he stared at the map, the video and timer flashed off and back on, both starting from the beginning. Tad couldn't help himself.

"Bullshit!" he screamed to no one.

That sound. Chair legs shuddering and scraping across a floor, but as loud as a jet engine. The door opened and out comes Asshole Golfer. Tad squares up. He's young and quick himself, but not negative percent body fat like this jerk. Or trained by the military. Everyone roundhouses who doesn't know how to fight, he thinks. So, he fakes with his right and throws a straight jab with his left. But this guy is down below him so quickly. From a knee, the man throws that straight, right jab directly into Tad's balls.

When Tad uncurls from his embryonic position on the walkway, the Asshole Golfer is long gone. But the pain in Tad's balls will continue for almost an hour. A cold, hollow throbbing sprinkled with little stabbing pains. He lays on the sofa downstairs and falls asleep hungry and in pain, looking like a vampire who attacked a woman on her period.

Voices

During the night (he supposed it was night, but there were no windows, and they kept the lights on), he was startled awake. A voice directly behind him. He sat up and looked around. No one.

"Tad, I need you to listen. Listen, but don't say anything aloud because they're listening, Okay?"

"Okay," Tad said aloud.

"Dude. Don't speak aloud! They're always listening! Speak with your mind."

Tad said, "Okay." But this time, only on the inside.

"You remember tiny Tad?" asked the voice.

"Um, yeah," Tad said aloud again.

Another voice spoke up, "Who are you talking to?"

This voice was more commanding. Having been asleep a few seconds ago, Tad had no idea who these voices were or where they were coming from.

"No one," he lied.

"We can tell when you're lying," the commanding voice said. Could they?

"You see what I'm saying. Don't say anything aloud," a familiar voice said. Why was it so familiar?

Tad mind-answered, "Okay." Did they drug him?

"Look, tiny Tad had a tinier tad and so on. You can think of me as quantum Tad."

Tad started to put that together in his head and then stopped. It was too much.

"Holy shit," he said.

Quantum Tad said, "Listen, I know there's a lot of shit going down in the Macro, but this will cancel all that out. I just witnessed the double-slit experiment in person. Well, when I say witnessed, I mean experienced non-locally within the superposition itself. Anyway, the orientation and dimensionality of wave propagation affects observable phenomena, you know, like the interference patterns. Unless the wave propagation is orthogonal from a higher dimension. I mean, it's literally like Plato said, all you have to do is turn your "head," i.e. rotate your consciousness ninety degrees and you can see it all at once. I'm going to repair our little mishap and then I can focus on the big reveal to the Macros. This is going to change everything. People will forget all about war when they see.

"Not sure all what you said, but it sounds... Hey, what mishap?" Tad asked quantum Tad.

"Oh. Well. I was depressed for a while, then found a restful state inside a static kind of melancholy, then transcended a pervasive and all-encompassing sadness to a suicidal state, during which I replaced all neutrinos with tiny books."

"Um, what?" Tad asked.

"It sounds bad, but worst-case scenario, the sun burns out a little early. I mean, none of the strong forces have been affected. Except maybe anywhere there's sand. But not the sand itself. The sand is fine."

"But... you can fix it?"

"Sure."

Tad realized that when someone answers in the affirmative with the word "sure," that person is tired of talking to you. Since there was nothing he could do to help with neutrinos, he decided the conversation was over, but being as the conversation was taking place inside his mind and on the quantum level, there was no real way to hang up.

He mind-said, "Okay... bye?"

Quantum Tad said, "Yeah, bye."

It was very weird to be finished with a conversation and not *do* something.

Tad lie on the sofa and thought about smaller and smaller Tads, like never-ending Russian dolls. He questioned why his parasitic marine friend hadn't taken up for him while he was getting pummeled. He thought, *nothing* makes sense anymore. Then he questioned the grammatical correctness of putting "anymore" at the end of that sentence. He thought of Strunk and White and fell asleep wondering from what nationality the name Strunk originated.

Morning Shower

Tad woke up and had to pee. He went over to the drainage tube in the corner, then stopped. He walked up the stairs and walked over to where the door slid open to let asshole golfers in to punch him.

He screamed, "Fuck you, asshole golfer, and fuck this place! And your mom's a hairy cunt!"

That should do it, he thought, and it did. The door slid open and as soon as Tad saw the pink Polo with the collar turned up, he threw his pants down a little, grabbed his junk, and shot a bladder-filled stream of piss all over the guy. The man stood his ground but turned his head. Tad knew something bad would happen next but didn't care. He had hit him directly on the side of the face. Piss dripped from his chiseled chin and his shirt and pants were soaked in spots.

Tad pulled up his pants and stared back, defiant. The man slowly turned his head back and looked at Tad for a few moments. As they continued their stare-off, Tad could see other men in regular fatigues at computers. He was on display. A military experiment. They wanted to see what came out when he was pissed. He knew this, and so the best way to get this over was to antagonize them back, get punished, and increase the rage. He would play their dumb fucking games.

But the man in front of him didn't throw a fist this time. He did something much worse. He smiled, albeit almost imperceptibly, then reached over and pressed a button that closed the door.

"Dickhead!" Tad screamed at the door. "Let me know when you need another morning shower."

The door remained shut and Tad turned to look at the glass box and then the couch below. That was really all there was to do. That and get dick punched. He was starving. Not really, but like American chubby starving.

"Fucking pricks," he mumbled to himself as he walked over to the glass box. He hated to comply with these assholes, but he could feel a headache coming on and hadn't drunk anything in some time. Unless he wanted to start drinking his own urine, he would have to play the game. The simple fact that this might be on the table passed through his mind as a very real possibility. He walked into the box and the video popped up, frozen and waiting on the glass in front of him. The timer also popped up, but this time it said four hours instead of two.

Country Music and Christmas Lights

Tad watched people sucker punched on the streets, a leopard run into someone's yard and grab a dog by its neck and drag it away while the owner screamed, and someone fall from a mountainside while hiking with some sherpa, their friends watching but not being able to help. Some videos were just an image that someone posted and the comments scrolling by. One of a girl, age nine, in her dress, getting ready for a dance. The comments were a mix of goodwill and hate. One girl told her to kill herself. The next thing on the screen was an article about the girl's suicide. He knew not to look away and steeled himself as he began to cry, head forward, watching as one thing after another assaulted his eyes and mind.

He glanced fleetingly at the clock. Thirty minutes left. He was going to make it. He watched players grab another player's hair and throw them to the ground, the referee doing nothing. A young, shirtless guy with a buzz cut telling him counterintuitive health advice because he was the only one with the secret to health. A string of fails where the person gets seriously injured. Fifteen minutes left.

Then ten full minutes of Christmas lights set to country music. Five minutes left. The map behind the videos on the wall updating. Did another country turn red? He forced himself to not look, to only focus on the video. An old lady holding her hands together, moving them back and forth while anxiously watching a computer screen. The back of her head was blocking the screen in front of her. She was in some type of contemporary house.

She turned her head and said, "Please, please let me speak to him! What's going on? Why is this happening?"

At the same moment he recognized the voice, she turned again, tears streaming down her face. Tad was on her computer monitor, getting up after being punched.

She pleaded with whoever was offscreen, "Please tell me why you're hurting my son! Please!"

Shrimp and Grits

Tad's face was set. His body rigid. The counter had reached zero and both the timer and the video switched off. The door opened to his left, but he did not move. Nor did he move a muscle when the plate of shrimp and grits was set before him and the asshole golfer said, "Enjoy."

When the man turned around, Tad shoved five of the larger shrimp on his plate into his mouth, chewing as hard and violently as he'd ever chewed anything, until it was a paste of saliva and mush. He thrust his hands into the plate and grabbed two handfuls of still piping hot grits and sausage and roux. He then slung both as hard as he could at the back of the man. The two clumps formed an arc mid-air that centered the man's back and head, the other flying over his head and through the opening of the open door. The man hunched his shoulders and turned.

Tad walked slowly towards him, hands up. Look, his face said, that was a moment of anger. I'm good now. I just want to—. And when he was a few feet from him, Tad made to tackle the man, proper American football style, with his shoulder in the man's side, wrapping up. He knew he would fail, but that wasn't the point. The man braced himself and got his bearings, and this was when Tad spit all the shrimp into his left hand and shoved it down the front of the man's pants.

Something hard split his shoulder apart and he fell to the walkway but then used every last drop of his will to rock back to his hands and knees, then roll backwards until he was in squatting position. He pulled his pants down.

Four hours is a lot of time to think. Think about things like that nagging question of why his buddy didn't have his back when he was getting the crap beat out of him, but would kill the shit out of doctors for seemingly no reason. And what he'd come up with is that his buddy did have his back. He would likely protect Tad if it came to life or death, but it hadn't. Tad just had a bloody nose. Nothing to go alien apeshit over.

But there is one rule that all of life on Earth shares, and that's *don't fuck with my food*. Tad was reminded of this as he watched a lion that was trying to take a hyena's food get attacked by the whole pack at one time. It never had a chance. It's the same for humans. Try taking someone's food off their plate in a restaurant. Any difference in size won't matter. There'll be a fight. That spawned him to remember those few pieces of shrimp that he saw when momentarily awakened during his procedure back at the hospital. Those doctors had somehow been seen as competitors. Weak, fleshy, human ones.

It was painful to stand. His shoulder felt like someone had hit it with a hammer, and he supposed that was an apt comparison. The asshole golfer was screaming. Tad turned to see the man's white golfing pants bulge in an array of strange contortions and then turn red. The dickhead back peddled, trying to get away from the blender in his pants. Someone behind him yelling to close the door as he fell backward through it. The door slid and stopped, hitting the man's legs that were still in the doorway, and reopened. More people screaming in the room beyond the doorway.

Tad sat on the stairs and stared at the map. There was a lot of red on the map. He assumed the red was controlled by the opposing forces. He supposed if he could help, then he needed to. But his mom? They needed to understand that moms were off-limits. Period.

After about ten minutes, he watched his little ass-buddy strobe through the door, still closing and reopening on the dead asshole's legs, and make its way beside him on the walkway.

He watched it intently and it appeared to regard him for a moment. Then it squirted out a chrysalis onto the walkway, which immediately hatched a worm. The worm arched like it was getting out of bed and yawning, then stretched into an egg-shaped, black object. *What is it with egg-shaped things?* His alien friend strobed into his butthole as he reached out and grabbed the black egg. He couldn't tell if it was metal or ceramic, or some weird hybrid.

Tad wasn't a gamer, but his roommate had been. He'd seen and heard the toxicity both while watching Ravi and in the glass box. Tad knew this black egg was his ticket out of here.

Good News

The general yelled tentatively through the room of dead soldiers. He and a squad of twenty men were at the room's other open door. He yelled again, "Mr. Gruber?"

Tad ignored him. Turned his newly hatched way out of this shithole over in his hand. How much did it weigh? How far could he throw it?

The door slid closed in front of the general. He said, "Really? We can't just keep any of the doors open? In a multi-billion-dollar installation, the doors open, wait five seconds, and then close? That's the only functionality built-in?"

One of the men reached over and placed his hand on the plate glass and the door opened for the fifth time. The man said, "Yes, sir."

"Awesome," the general said, and walked through the doorway, stepping over and around the dead men, and leaned over to look through the door that led to the walkway. He could see Tad sitting at the top of the stairs. He waved his hands at the men following him. Put down your weapons and stay. One of the men did not comply. What the hell was it with people?

"Soldier, look at your fellow soldiers. Look in this man's hands and what's lying next to that one over there. Tell me what you see."

The nervous man surveyed the room as instructed, quickly, with his eyes on the doorway. All the dead men had emptied guns lying next to them. The soldier finally lowered his. As he did so, the general motioned to another soldier and said, "Get him the fuck out of here."

He turned back to the hallway and about shit himself. Tad was standing almost in the doorway, but just out of view of the other men.

Tad said, "General."

"Look, we're in a hurry and overstepped our boundaries," the general said, placating hands in front of him.

"Overstepped? My mom. Lemme tell you somethin—"

"No, no, no, no. Look." The general motioned for one of the men to access a computer. Then motioned for Tad to come into the room, and for the first time, saw the object in Tad's hand. "Show him both," he ordered the soldier.

On the screen, the video of his mom came up, but it was off somehow. The movements. The color. The soldier pointed at her hand and said, "The fingers. See? This is an earlier version. AI, nothing more. No moms were harmed in the... making..."

He was going to say 'of this' but the humor fell flat in the room. Tad could see it was indeed AI-generated.

"That was an early version. You saw the polished one. This is the real one."

Tad's mom came up again. She was watching one of her westerns. She got up and walked to the kitchen and in a moment came back. That almost imperceptible limp from rolling her ankle almost a decade ago.

The general said, "Your mom is fine. Safer than half the planet right now. But that's only right now."

Tad turned from the screen to the general, who continued.

"You can see the map, son. They have people like you... hosts. But they got a head start. Our methods may have been misguided, but if our projections are correct, our methods won't mean shit to anyone in about two months, because we'll all be gone or under their cold, steel boots."

"One-hour shifts, not four. You can give me drugs that'll keep me irritated, fuck with the temperature, whatever, but food that doesn't make me gag and a toilet."

The general said, "Done. And um... do you know what that is?"

Tad walked into the room and put out his hand. The general reached out and gingerly took the egg-shaped object from Tad.

Tad said, "How long would you say it would take to get to the surface right now?"

The general looked a little apprehensive. "Oh, about two and a half minutes, I'd guess. Why?"

"Well, sir. Because I'm *still* pissed about what happened," Tad said, reaching forward and taking the egg, twisting it until it clicked, and putting it back in the general's hand, "I'm going say you've got about five minutes to get this to the surface. Just a guess."

The general stared wide-eyed at the now blinking red object in his hand. "Goddamnit, Tad!" he said, turning and walking quickly out of the room. He didn't run as he very much did not want to trip with whatever this was in his hand. As he rounded the corner of the hallway, he saw the soldier he banished from the room. The man started to apologize, but the general put the blinking egg in his hands and clamped them together. His smile was wide.

"Son, you're a scared little shit of a man, and right now that's exactly what we need. I'd say you have less than two minutes to get this top side and far away from the entry. Not sure what happens after that, but I would hurry."

The man stood, looking between his fingers at the pulsing object. Then he looked up at the general and soldier who had taken him from the room. Then he ran.

"Son!" the general hollered. The man turning around in a panic. The general pointing in the correct direction.

"Shit! Sorry!" the man exclaimed and ran.

He motioned for the soldier that was left to walk with him back to his quarters and followed a private hallway to an elevator. They got on and it raced upward. The doors opened and the soldier followed the general through an abandoned room to the outside, which was incredibly bright. They marched around a silo and an old brick building until the other soldier recognized the main entranceway to the facility. The general looked at his watch. If the idiot didn't make it, he was hopefully far enough above to be safe.

After a few moments, the panicked soldier ran through the old door and looked around. When he saw the general and the other soldier had beat him to the surface, he froze, a deer in headlights. The general pointed south, away from not only the entrance but the underground portions of the facility as well. The man sprinted, no longer clutching the egg with both hands, but toting it like a baseball so he could get his hands into the run. The general began walking in the man's direction, glancing at his watch. After the man was a good hundred yards away, he turned and waved to the general, who in turn waved for him to keep going, making a thing of pointing at his watch.

You've got time. Run.

Another hundred yards and the man stopped. You could hear the high-pitched whining, even at this distance. The flashing rhythm increased to almost one continuous red light. The man threw the egg as hard as he could. Then he turned and ran as fast as he could. For about ten feet.

The sound was a bottle rocket going off underwater. There was no flash of light or explosive sound. The general could see that where there used to be tarmac and sand in front of him, most of it was gone now. He followed the lack of ground to directly in front of him. Looking down, he realized he was on a precipice.

After the ground disappeared, the wind picked up and was blowing even harder now. Enough to push the general over the edge. It was more of a prolonged slide than a fall, but certainly disorienting to say the least. He looked at the soldier above him and then all around. It was a perfectly concave crater, about three hundred yards wide he guessed, and almost as deep. He was about fifty feet down one side. He stomped his heels into the curve of dirt until it compacted, giving him a steady foothold, then stood and looked out across the devastation.

This was good news. Very good news, indeed.

You Okay?

The general relayed the good news to Tad, who was in his new room within the hour. He would eat twice a day and watch the horrible feeds for an hour at a time. They were adding things to the food that would crank things up. And indeed, Tad started dropping close to five eggs a day. After a week, the general came in and they walked down to his old digs, where the map on the wall looked a little different. There were some blue and green spots in the middle of the red areas.

The general pointed to one of the green ones and said, "That's you, man. That's ours now. Turns out they're not metallic and slide right past metal detectors. They didn't know what the hell hit them. Their whole headquarters evaporated. They abandoned the surrounding area. I think we took out one of their hosts as well. No more lava storms in the area after that."

"Awesome. Hey, I'm shitting like ten of these a day now. How much longer do you think?"

The general looked away, then back again. "Well, there are no deadlines in war, son."

"Yeah," Tad said. "Makes sense."

"Look, we tried to figure out a way to make this not so unpleasant, but tuuuh..."

"It's kind of the point. Yeah, I get it."

There wasn't much more to say, so Tad walked back to his room. He now had a toilet and bed, though the bed sagged in the middle and he always woke up with his back hurting. There were other mild inconveniences purposefully geared to irritate the shit out of him. They were always watching. Especially if he was watching the socials. He was certain his poker face was unknowable, but they always seem to catch when he was particularly disgusted with something. They would repeat it multiple times during the hour-long process.

He was watching a bear attempt to run across a highway for the fifth time today. A short clip, but seeing the poor thing get hit and slide across the pavement over and over made him want to slather whoever created this program in honey and leave them in the jungle, buried up to their neck.

He was in the middle of watching this poor thing and then he was watching a cowboy ride up to a ranch house. He was also sitting down. On a couch. He didn't move his head for a minute as he took it all in. The living room and kitchen. The fireplace. The TV. His mom sitting next to him.

"You okay?" she asked him. "You look stiff as a board for some reason."

Tad was indeed as stiff as a board. Because he was in an underground installation watching horrible socials and shitting bombs and now he was in a room with his mom watching a western. There was no segue. No transition whatsoever. He finally managed to turn his head and look at her.

"I'm fine," he told her.

Her face screwed up a little and she said, "You don't look fine. And why are you smiling all weird?"

And indeed, as Tad thought about it, that bougie Cashmore smile had probably worn off on him a little too easily.

"I don't know. But hey, Greenland is nice, right?" He didn't know what to say and looking around, he couldn't tell where they were. It was dark outside and the house exuded a mix of contemporary Hansel and Gretel.

"Greenland?" she said, looking even more incredulous.

"You're in Minnesota," a voice said.

"Minnesota?" Tad repeated aloud.

"Are you guessing?" his mom asked. "Are you having a stroke or something?"

The voice said, "Oh my god. Will you stop talking aloud?"

Tad tried to smile correctly at his mom this time. He said, "Oh, okay," on the inside.

Quantum Tad said, "Oh shit! I'll be right back. You're freaking out!"

Tad said aloud, "I am? Uh, okay."

His mom stared at him. "You're not on something, are you?"

"You'll be good for a second," quantum Tad said. "We swapped you out. Also, this mom seems pretty cool. Do you like her okay?"

Tad looked to his left, then back again.

Pink Elephant

On the inside, Tad said, "What did you do to me?"

"We swapped you out with another you."

"So... another me is in the installation?"

"Yes, we tried prepping you with a little conversation and explanations beforehand, but you thought you were schizophrenic or something. So, we told you to just watch the horrible things and we would put you back in an hour. But I mean, we don't have to. You've been through a lot and this mom is slightly more agreeable."

Tad sat still for a moment more until his mom pretended to start watching TV again, but she was certainly watching him from the corner of her eye.

"Okay, so what if this guy freaks out and... wait... whaddya mean you don't have to put me... him... back and what... wait, this is not my original mom?"

"Well, I mean, there's an infinity of your moms. And they're all your moms, so..."

Tad made his mind whisper louder for an angry and confused effect.

"Hey! Hey. Listen. I'm sure this lady is nice and all, but I want my original mom and not doppelgänger mom."

"Well, we can't swap moms, or anyone else for that fact. Only you, because we're connected at the quantum level. I mean, there's a little decoherence here and there, but nothing like with the sand. So, you want to go back then?"

Tad took a moment to think about that, then felt immediately ashamed for even thinking about leaving his OG mom in another, what, spacetime? Not only that but thinking about this other Tad, who maybe had no parasite, used to hanging out with his mom and chillin, suddenly being thrown into *his* nightmarish world, well, that seemed a bit much. Like something a comic book villain would do.

"Um, yes. Of course! And what's with the sand—"

And just like that Tad was staring at a rapey comment on someone's feed, and another Tad sat on his mom's couch, staring wide-eyed at the TV and exclaiming in a loud and concerned voice, "Well, holy shit!"

Tad felt bad, but after no less than thirty seconds, he said inwardly, "Okay, maybe just for the rest of this hour's watch," and he was back in front of the TV, his mom standing next to the sofa now, squinting at him.

She said, "An installation? Baby, what are you talking about? You're starting to worry me."

Tad looked at her and said, "I'm fine," and then realizing his situation continued with, "What do we have to eat?"

Moms always wanted to feed you.

"Goulash. You want taters or rice?" she asked, still searching his face for clues to the sudden outburst.

Tad smiled his bougie smile, which made his mom even more uneasy.

"Taters."

His mom watched him devour his food like he hadn't eaten in years. During this process, Tad couldn't stop thinking about how quantum Tad could not only put him into any spacetime he wanted but also, apparently, leave him there. This was slightly terrifying. But why worry if it was Tad himself, right? But then, how well did Tad know himself? He then realized that quantum Tad was probably always listening and tried not to think about it. He immediately thought of a pink elephant.

Growing up Black in the 1950s

Tad popped back into the installation in time to see the video and timer end. He walked over to the custom contraption they had built for him to lay his eggs from and leaned forward, kicking his legs back into the stirrups. This somehow facilitated more eggs. He heard way more than ten hit the floor. He didn't want to look. It was so many, and he would rather his friend have popped out and laid them for him, then strobed back inside, but you know, wish in one hand...

He looked down at a sea of black eggs. And one book? He removed himself from the contraption and pulled up his shorts. Tad picked up the book as the handlers came in to collect the eggs. He wiped the slime from the outside so he could make out the tiny title.

Growing up Black in the 1950s
by Tad Gruber, et al.

Tad spoke to the handlers, one of whom was Black, and said, "I'll hold on to this for a bit."

The Black handler turned to the other for some sort of validation. The other handler said, "They told us to collect the eggs. Didn't say anything about books." They both shrugged and finished collecting.

Tad couldn't get past the first twenty pages that night. He didn't want to think about why or how this book was formed. It was uninformed and low-key racist. Tad had no idea what it was like to be Black, now or decades ago, and the book was so cringe that he got up to throw it in the fireplace, but realized there was no fireplace and sat back down on the bed. Then his eyes were shut and when he opened them, he was staring at his other mom's TV. She was asleep on the couch, and he supposed he had been as well only a moment ago.

He didn't appreciate the shift with no warning, but there was now a fireplace to get rid of the book in. Tad took notice that the book was still in his hand, so he supposed quantum Tad had—

"Yeah, that wasn't easy, but we pulled it through," quantum Tad said with an air of accomplishment.

Tad got up quietly, so as not to disturb his mom, even though there was a shootout happening on the TV, and walked over to the fireplace with the book. He glanced at it one more time and unceremoniously tossed it into the fire. When it hit the flames, a wailing erupted that Tad could not fathom and he jumped backward, taking several steps away and then falling back onto the sofa.

"Holy shit!" he exclaimed.

He wasn't sure what was happening. Had the books been alive this whole time? Living organisms? The wailing continued for a second and then stopped. He had killed something. A living thing.

Tad heard laughing inside his head.

"I am so, so sorry. That was spur of the moment. Couldn't resist. My apologies," quantum Tad giggled.

It took a moment for Tad to realize quantum Tad had been the one wailing.

Tad was breathing heavily as he looked at his other mom, who was now awake and had her serious face on. She said, "You're not hanging out with that wild bunch this weekend. You can stay here, or we can go to the doctor right—"

Tad was back on his installation bed, lying on his side, eyes closed.

The other Tad awoke on his sofa to find his mom chastising him. "Did you hear me, young man?"

No. He had not.

Tad's nerves were shot, but his belly felt as if it was still full of good food. He drifted off and slept like a baby for the first time in months.

A Critique

Tad caught the warm, buttery smells from the restaurant's kitchen. He dipped his torn piece of bread in a mix of olive oil, melted butter, and balsamic glaze. The smorgasbord of flavors melted gently in his mouth as his eyes poured over the book's final pages. A denouement so concisely and deftly bound to his unique sense of catharsis that he felt momentarily empty of emotion or desire for further knowledge. Tad closed the book and took a drink of lemon water.

He sat and contemplated the method the author used to introduce the terroir of art within the confines of Capitalism and men's never-ending desire to destroy, he wanted to say each other, but really it was everything that wasn't them. The foreign. The Other. Unless of course, they could be put to plow.

It could be said that the delivery mechanism was too absurd and chaotic, but isn't that what life was? A syrupy ocean of pandemonium and farcical indifference to which we are born at the sandy bottom and spend a lifetime desperately dogpaddling, in vain, to reach the surface. If the author had not chosen such a surreal setting, could it not be argued that the hyperbolically absurd actions of men would have allowed for a deeper juxtaposition than the reader could force upon their suspension of disbelief?

And even for an absurdist novella, he had to question the ending. He was so tired of *Endings Explained*. And though the author had reined in the ending just short of that, there was still room for interpretation. Wasn't that the main issue with things like religion and pizza? Too many interpretations? Of course, knotting the message too tightly would cut off the circulation to those wondrous spaces of the unknown we reserve for both horror and mystical fascination. Life's poetry is best when it's slipping through your fingers, allowing your grasp of it in small undetermined moments, and leaving a scar as it falls from your hands, one that you'll reflect on here and there during one of life's few serene pauses. So, he allowed for certain ranges of ambiguity in those final moments.

Tad paid his bill and gathered his satchel. He walked down the cobblestoned streets and gave thanks to the overcast day and light winds. The architecture here seemed more intricate than necessary, but it gave the eyes something to tangle with on long walks. A fleur-de-lis that extrapolated to a more random and filigree flora, or an arabesque mesh of tiles with that familiar, interwoven collage of blue snake-like symbols.

He opened the door to the bakery and was greeted by the workers as he turned the corner and sat at his desk. He was somewhat on display, as his desk was set sideways and only five or so feet from one of the bakery's front windows. People would stop every now and then and stare while he pecked away at his keyboard, himself unaware of their presence outside. It was a novelty of sorts, a conversation starter, or point of interest for bibliophiles. Some would say it was navel-gazing or solipsistic, but others would say it was voyeuristic in an innocent way to watch a local author write his next book. Would it be as successful as his last one?

Other Tads

Tad popped back in, watched the video and timer shut off, then got in his contraption and laid his eggs. Forty or so this time. Two months in and they had perfected the enzymes and his diet. Climbing out, he leaned over and picked up the one book that was still in the process of blooming.

He loved the way the heat of creative energy filled his hand. The thought of all those words being written in such a few short moments. The compressed magic that must go into that. He walked over to his sofa and sat down, wiping away the bright green goo. The title this time was *How to Raise the Dead Without Using Your Hands*. He laughed. That influence was from yesterday's shift. This Tad loved horror and watched a weird B Movie with friends about an entire church that got possessed during a sermon.

After a few months, he slipped into a sadness that grew daily, so he finally gave in and began swapping out with Tads during the glass box sessions. He was sure the military had caught his tunnelling on camera. There was a book in his hand that had disappeared after all. But they said nothing. Maybe they were afraid of getting an answer. Maybe they knew exactly what was happening. Who knew?

Shifting had surpassed its initial voyeuristic curiosity. Tad felt like a demon, possessing the bodies of unsuspecting Tads with lives seemingly better than his own. Tiny little, one time, short-term vacations to see how things could have been. It was exhilarating. And though it was his mind in another body, those existing neural pathways seemed to lend themselves to interaction. In this way, he was able to experience different forms of emotional satiety henceforth unavailable to him, as well as utilize existing knowledge and habits for his short-term benefit.

Today's shift had been quite enjoyable. He was a successful author whose life appeared void of struggle. Of course, no one's life was void of struggle, and he was certain if he could stay and look around, he would find some history of trauma in his earlier life. What else could explain the thoughts writers have?

Lucid Dreaming

Tad watched the first few minutes of the glass box feed before he was sitting on a dock. He took in his surroundings first. A placid lake, a house sitting behind him on a slight incline, and a boat in the distance, far enough away that you could barely hear its muffled engine chugging along. The sky was blue and red and orange and none of the colors were fighting. He wasn't certain if it was sunset or sunrise, but after a few moments there was less of the orange ball touching the lake. Sunset then. He was enjoying a sunset.

He wondered if there were any times where the other simply couldn't handle that hour shift after the fact.

Quantum Tad said, "Well, it certainly leaves an indelible mark on you. The first year is the worst. You're all jumpy and waiting for it to happen again. It creates a hypervigilant state that negatively impacts your state of mind and physical health. But over the years it attenuates."

"Over the years? It's only been a few months. How would you know what happens over the years?"

Quantum Tad usually had quick and well-formed answers. This was not one of those times. There were at least three seconds of silence. Then quantum Tad said, "Well, you know, time is slightly different where we are."

"Wait, do you already know what's going to happen? In... all instances of... Tad?"

No answer at all this time, even after ten seconds.

"Can you time travel?" Tad asked, then after thinking about it for a second, asked, "Am I time travelling right now? Or is this the same moment in... time?"

"Look, there are certain things better left alone. We don't mess with time."

It sounded to Tad like quantum Tad had put quotes around the word 'time' when he said it. This made Tad uncomfortable in ways he couldn't articulate.

He said, "Okay."

Quantum Tad changed the subject. "I'll tell you something interesting, though. In some of these instances, when you were taking a nap, you recalled the incident later as something that happened during sleep. A dreaming state where you were aware you were dreaming, but didn't immediately wake up, and could even 'control' the dream to some degree. Once it's discovered, the scientists in all these instances end up referring to it as lucid dreaming. They all call it the same thing. You'd think in an infinity of these discoveries, one of them would call it something else, right?"

The sun dipped below the water's horizon.

Tad said, "Wait a sec. Lucid dreaming has always been a thing. We've always had that term here. What does that mean?"

Tad peered out at the lake and sky. It was the bluing hour. The soft, diffused light coated everything in a liminal substance that both hid definition and brought out a higher relief at the same time. Quantum Tad's silence was louder than the silence of the lake.

Corporate Takeover

Tad's mom visited and stayed for a week. She had indeed been moved to Greenland and well taken care of. There was no more pretense after six months of World War. They showed her the map and, although they stopped short of explaining the gritty details, let her know that her son was playing a large part in keeping the red parts from spreading to the rest of the world. She asked if he was eating well, and everyone lied with straight faces. They showed her a staged room where Tad was supposedly living. Her son looked happy and he was doing an important job. She left happy herself and travelled back to Greenland.

Tad later pooped out two recipe books that were passed around the installation and deemed bestsellers via a whiteboard they kept on the wall of the command center. The book leaned heavily on seafood, with six different recipes for shrimp and grits. None of them contained andouille sausage.

During the seventh month, they brought in a host that was captured on the front lines. This freaked Tad out considerably. The front lines were four countries over, but the fact that he was somebody important enough for the other side to capture hit him for the first time. He'd never had to get close to the front lines, but had watched clips on the glass box and there was some wild shit going down out there. He was "happy" to stay here in the installation.

After the recipe books, he knew he needed to get back to the grind, so Tad forced himself to watch the entirety of the glass box feed. But today was different. The general came in and they took a walk down to his old digs. They stood in front of the giant projection on the wall and Tad could see the green and blue spots had shrunk considerably again. He sighed.

Tad said, "So what now?"

"Well, son. Things have gotten a little grim. We need to think outside the box. We've got some old friends from the auction just down the hall, as well as a captured host. We're going to try something a little bold."

The general told him the plan and Tad didn't flinch. He was past flinching. Past much anything. The drudgery of it all had encompassed him. He was watching and shifting up to six times a day now. Eggs were pouring out. The last day's count was a hundred and thirty-seven. He thought of the destruction that many eggs could cause and couldn't understand how they could be losing the war. But he wasn't going to let his mom down. And selfishly, he certainly didn't want to get captured by the enemy.

He walked into the room and saw the spider and snail hosts, along with another woman who looked bedraggled and scared. In the middle of the room was a piece of cabbage with a peeled banana on it, and next to that was a container of crickets. They all pulled their pants down and their parasites emerged. These parasites were much smaller than Tad's, and resembled a spider and a snail if they had fallen into a vat of toxic waste. It was a strange feeling to have at this point in time, but Tad had the first feeling of pride in his parasite. His was way cooler.

A soldier sprayed the spider man's parasite with fish sauce and another handler tossed some chunks of shrimp atop the snail. The captured host's parasite was futuristic, like out of some sci-fi movie. It was the same size as his, but looked like a robot with a million tiny parts. The general said it was an automaton, but not what it could do. They sprayed it as well.

The girl whose symbiosis was with the snail began crying and begging with the general. "No! Please! I like mine. We paint together. It helps me. Please!"

The general nodded and Tad squatted and pulled his pants down. His parasite strobed out and immediately attacked the other parasites in the room, consuming them in seconds.

They escorted the three hosts out. Seeing his octo-urchin attack and consume some type of futuristic bot was more disturbing than he thought it would be, not just because of the brutal, animalistic quality of the attack, and not because of the surreal nature of it all; he'd become used to all manner of weirdness. It was the fact that his parasite more than doubled in size. He didn't want to think about what would be happening to his butthole when it strobed back inside him. And there were the unknowns connected to the interactions that just happened between parasites.

Now the size of a large microwave, his slimy author friend disappeared behind him and, unlike before, he felt a slight discomfort as it slithered inside him.

There was no downtime. They moved him to the glass box and he watched an hour of socials and feeds and news from around the world. Then he climbed into his contraption, which they had for some reason modified. It now had padding, as well as a lot of other moving parts that he couldn't see a use for yet.

He waited and waited. He hovered over the floor in the same position he had for months, like a person straddling an invisible jet ski, and bent his head down to see what would come out.

When he was younger, at a birthday party his mom forced him to attend for a boy he didn't get along with, they had handed out these plastic things that looked like tiny bottles with a string. They had all pulled the strings at the same time. There was a loud POP! and confetti filled the room.

This is what Tad saw happen below him. An explosion of colorful, confetti-like objects. The difference was that these weren't pieces of paper. He knew this because they flew around the room. Some landed on the walls or floors and crawled around. These were the most brightly colored flying spiders he had ever seen.

Eggs started pouring from him. Almost a continuous stream of much smaller eggs. These eggs weren't black and scary, but multicolored, like Easter eggs. There were hundreds rolling around below him. How can that much stuff come out of me, he thought.

The flying spiders swooped down and attached to the eggs and lifted them into the air. The door to the room opened and they all flew their payloads out of the room.

"Okay," Tad said. "That was different."

He grabbed the bars atop his contraption with his hands and began to pull his feet and legs out of his stirrups, but he couldn't get them out. Confused, he looked down to see what was catching his legs. He knew immediately what it was, but chose to ignore the obvious, until he looked up to see metallic straps around his forearm as well.

"Guys?" he said to the aether.

The general said, "Hey, Tad."

So back to Tad. No Mr. Gruber or son. That wasn't good.

"What are we doing?"

"Well, just being honest, we had no idea what would happen, so we had to take precautions."

Tad could hear the wind on the general's microphone.

"Are you guys all top side?"

A moment of hesitation before the general said, "Yeah."

"Um, okay. I need out. I'm done for now guys."

"Well, Tad...," the general sounded apologetic. "We've had to ramp things up. I mean, look, we're at the point that we really need to give one last push over the next few weeks to end this war. We're going to have to let this play out, son."

Tad gripped his bar and shook his legs violently, smashing his ankle into some metal and screaming in pain, then did the same with his arms. It was useless. He wasn't going anywhere.

The general continued, "Son, we don't know exactly what you're doing when you zone in and out, but it seems it's affecting the integrity of the product. Some of the eggs don't work as expected. We detonated a few in a really important location and there was no quiet vaporization of matter. It did cover the area in a protracted and inescapable melancholy that eventually led to a surrender, but most of the subjects had already committed suicide, so we couldn't extract any information. We need you turned on and tuned in."

"Fine! Let me out of here! I'll stop distracting myself from... the rage bait. I'll stay pissed."

The general sighed. "I believe you, son. But we have to make sure of that. For the sake of the country."

"Holy shit! Guys! You can't just leave me in this thing!?"

There was no answer. Tad pictured the empty rooms in the facility and all the men standing around up top, watching him squirm. He was so pissed he couldn't think. And that's exactly what they wanted.

A Tiny Prison Called the Self

The German chef stood with hands on hips, the so-called Superman stance. A way to draw power into oneself. He was on the veranda and could feel the mist from the ocean in the light gusts of wind. The view every morning was astounding. Not ten years ago, he was looking out at a dirty rooftop and a rusty access door through a tiny window from his tiny apartment. Now all he had to do was fix a few dishes every day and he lived like a king. He had caught himself getting used to his circumstances when he was handpicked and whisked away to this paradise. It only took a couple of weeks. But this made him feel weird, because he knew circumstances can change on a dime. So, each morning he walked out on the veranda and, while watching the sunrise, purposefully recalled things from his not so wonderful past life. This kept him thankful and in a good place.

Since he had spent years in a cramped apartment with other restaurant employees, he understood tiny Tad's inability to deal with his current circumstances. Tiny Tad was trapped in a prison not of his making. A tiny prison called the Self. It was outlandish to say the least, and if he hadn't stood there face to face with tiny Tad, he would never have believed it himself. But come what may, you had to face your demons lest they consume you. The German chef had intimate knowledge of this.

After macro Tad left, things had slid steadily downhill for tiny Tad. It turned out that he did, indeed, have a tiny version of the parasite. The first micro Tad was only a couple inches tall. And whereas tiny Tad was drenched in melancholy, micro Tad was consumed by paranoia and fear. He kept on and on about dust mites. Said they looked like spider ticks and were everywhere.

After consulting with Cashmore, he was able to acquire equipment to house and take care of both tiny and micro Tads. He also directed the chef to give tiny Tad some of the Jello in his food to increase production for a few weeks. This increased tiny Tad's dread and the chef felt bad about doing it, but remembered his own tiny apartment and how easily he could end up back in it, then complied.

Micro Tads were everywhere. They clustered in groups and discussed their plight. There were often mental breakdowns and screaming, but you could hardly hear them so it wasn't so bad. Tiny Tad, however, could hear them fine and bore the brunt of their frustrations. He began spiraling. He wept. Disappeared for days at a time and turned up looking ragged and gaunt.

The chef talked with tiny Tad and promised to take care of the situation if he agreed. Tiny Tad was reluctant, but acquiesced in the end as he could take no more. The chef then gathered all the micro Tads up so he could take them to a facility more suited to their size. They would be happier there.

He called Cashmore and related what he and tiny Tad had decided. The Jello had worked and there were over a hundred micro Tads that were impossible to take care of. He wasn't sure why Cashmore had chosen to add fuel to the fire by creating more of a problem. But people like Cashmore always had a plan to turn profit, even in the darkest of times.

The sun had risen above the ocean's horizon and the glass-like water was slowly beginning to undulate and rise to meet the day's expectations. The German chef smiled and returned to the kitchen. The clear Lexan tub sat on the stainless steel countertop. There were holes in the top for air. They were all pressed against one side like they were at a concert but backed away quickly when he entered the room. There was a tiny din of barely audible protests as he removed the top.

He added a pinch of salt to the boiling water and a tablespoon of extra virgin olive oil. The Lexan was greased so they couldn't scale the sides. The chef watched their pale skin redden as they plunged into the roiling water. After parboiling, he removed their home-stitched pullovers and arranged them on the mesh. He removed the hair, sometimes taking the scalp as well. That was okay; this was a rustic presentation. The basting sauce was a balsamic glaze of his own creation, black as a prison guard's humor. His brush gently caressed them from the neck down, leaving the head exposed. He then skewered ten at a time, piercing them in the side like the Christ our Lord.

When he got the signal from Cashmore, the chef rolled the trolley into the dining room. There were five people on each side of the table, each with their own grill and mix of coconut shell charcoal and Binchotan. Cashmore gave his speech as oohs and ahhs filled the air, the crowd mesmerized by their own privilege to be invited to such a closed circle and taboo event.

The chef circled the table three times. On the first pass, he arranged the micro Tads face down with their heads just off the edge of the grill. On the second pass, he turned them over, and on the third pass he placed them on the virgin white platters in front of his amazed guests, stepping back against the wall to remove himself from the very experience he created, but remaining in the room in case there were questions.

"Oh my God!" one of them said. "That's really him."

"Were you there? At the auction? I couldn't make it," another exclaimed.

"You didn't use any peanuts, did you?" asked another.

Another seemed displeased that no one else was praying over their food.

A man in a bright purple suit was already on his third, eating them whole with exuberance, as a shy lady in a black dress asked about their emotional journey to the table.

A man who could have been easily mistaken for Hemingway was saying it was easier if you held them by the head, like so.

"How is your water filtered?" one asked.

The German chef smiled and answered all their questions with verve and delight. A nod from Cashmore and he returned to the kitchen. He moved the embers around on his own grill as he thought about the money already in his bank account. He could now go anywhere he liked and live anywhere he wanted. And he would. He would build a house with wide open areas and large windows that looked out on the most beautiful vistas. He would watch sunrises from his own veranda and not have to think of where he came from anymore. Because he would never go back to that place.

The chef smiled and left the kitchen to go and find tiny Tad. He was famished.

Dubbed Anime

Parts of Tad sagged around the contraption's parts. He didn't know how much he weighed now, but it was probably double what he had weighed a couple of years ago. Gravity pulled the huge sections of fat down and stretched his skin like a rubber band that would never snap back. The contraption rolled him over and a tube descended to within a couple of inches of his mouth.

In the beginning, he had railed against the automatons. Did the opposite of everything they wanted. All for naught. If he didn't open his mouth, take in the gruel and swallow, then the tube would slide down his throat, emptying itself into his belly anyway. The gruel made him gag. They knew this, of course. Because they consistently showed him videos of how hotdogs were made after he made the disgusting connection between the color and consistency of his daily feedings and a video he'd once seen.

There were thousands and thousands of automatons. There was nothing they couldn't do. Rebuild his contraption on the fly and transfer him to the new one in mid-air. Prepare his gruel. Yesterday, one of the colorful spiders landed on the glass that sat a few inches below his face at all times and caused the video feed to flicker. Other times one would cause distortions in color or horizontal lines to randomly jam the screen. They didn't show socials during this time, but videos he was interested in. The volume either way to loud or so soft you couldn't make out what they were saying. The only thing worse, they sometimes showed anime or movies that were dubbed.

A slow but steady stream of eggs fell from his anus, about one every ten seconds. Once the automatons realized he was numb to whatever happened on his backside, they injected him with all sorts of different things until they found something that made him regain his pain receptors. It wasn't excruciating, just highly annoying. His pee was recirculated and filtered. He could see all this happening in front of his eyes. The tubes filling with yellow and dripping slowly through a filter into another clear container that led to his mouth. Like a hamster, he could reach his head over slightly and suck the water out of a tube when he was thirsty. Sometimes, they would let the filter go bad for a few days before changing it.

Last week, a news video was shown on the screen in front of him. It was an inaugural celebration of the war's end. The war had been won thanks to some new technology the military was using that simply erased whatever matter was within a few hundred yards of it. This show of power had been enough to cause revolts in the enemy countries, and then civil wars in others. This led eventually to surrenders and the start of the treaty signing process. Things had been peaceful for the last year and a half.

He stared at the screen. It had all happened well over a year ago. Tad began to weep. As he did, a needle punctured his arm and liquid flowed into his helpless, flabby body. The custom mix of meth and ketamine caused an immediate, baseless euphoria. He was both hyper-focused and detached, his thoughts fragmented and his fight or flight response activated while in a deep, mental paralysis. He floated through a nauseating psychosis. And though it was terrifying and left him hollow, he would immediately crave it again the next day. A reprieve from this private hell, fleeting though it was.

Impotent Voyeurism

"Hey. Quantum Tad! I know you're there. C'mon, dude. Please!"

Following a moment of silence, Tad made to hang his head in defeat. Of course, he couldn't because his chin was resting on a pad so he could view the screen 24/7. Looking away from the screen was frowned upon. In a big way. But then a voice rumbled through his anxious mind.

"Yes?"

This voice was different. Deeper. Slower. Sullen even?

"Is this Quantum Tad? Man, you... uh, sound different."

The screen showed a clip of someone driving through a crowd of people in the street, some going up and over the car, and at least one person going under.

"No," came the answer.

The voice reverberated, off what he would never know. But one word answers were not in Quantum Tad's wheelhouse. He seemed to always be hyped up on Quantum Cocaine when he was talking to Tad. He almost didn't want to ask the next, obvious question.

"Who is this?"

On the screen police swarmed a high school campus, a line of crying children being led to safety.

Another extended pause.

"I'm what you might call elemental Tad."

Well, that sounds ominous.

"Okay. Look, I'm a little freaked out right now. I'm sure you can see my situation. I just need to shift out to a better experience. I mean, not for good, just here and there to give myself a break. I don't want to screw another Tad over, but just... There was this one Tad who's a famous writer. Maybe we could swap here and there? I can't do this constantly, all day, every day, for the rest of my life. I'm producing a massive amount here. Surely there's some reprieve."

"Quantum Tad handles Adjacent shifts and he is in a funk at the moment, one from which I'm not certain he can remove himself."

"But... But he said he had a solution to the war and—"

"Quantum Tad is perpetually overwhelmed with possibilities. While he can see them all at once, his ability to settle on one in particular is constrained by his rather liminal mindset. He blames you for this."

"What?" Tad exclaimed as he stared at an image of a modern-day woman tied up and waiting to be sold as a slave. "What did I do?"

"You are responsible for his creation. Your increased insecurity and repressed sadness spawned an ever shrinking chain of neurotic Tads."

Tad said, "Holy shit, man. I didn't mean to. I was only trying to make myself better by taking a good, long look at myself.

Tad thought about never being able to shift to an Adjacent, and how insanity wasn't just doing the same thing over and over again and expecting things to magically get better, it was also when you could no longer distract yourself from the reality of this. But then, if distractions are all we have to stave off insanity, but the distractions themselves lead to insanity, how to break the cycle?

The screen showed middle schoolers fighting. One bragging after knocking another out with one punch.

Elemental Tad said, "You are rather lucky. In his anger and disillusionment, quantum Tad could have placed you in any number of Adjacents that are much worse. Instead, his hopelessness has tamped down his infinity of possibilities. His lack of hope in bettering his own situation has led to a staggering degree of apathy. You understand, he has access to all the most wondrous propagations of Tad, one of which you have spent time in, but can only live vicariously through a larger version. He is confined to an eternity of impotent voyeurism, always aware of the possibilities of a good life, but never the agency to attain it."

The screen showed the bear again, sliding across the pavement.

He said, "So... You're like the root Tad. Can't you do something?"

"I could, but it would be nonsensical. I am the root from which all Tad variations propagate. Every possible variation in every possible Adjacent will, and has, occurred. Change doesn't make sense if all possible changes are already accounted for. If it's any consolation, Tads swap with each other almost every second or two, but only in very similar Adjacents, so it goes mostly unnoticed."

Tad thought, *at the root of existence, there is only indifference.*

The screen showed the bear again, sliding across the pavement.

Tad mind-spoke, "I just want to sit in front of my window again and write."

The screen showed the bear again, sliding across the pavement.

It was cold today in the installation.

Tad spoke to the aether, "I would like a warm blanket."

Acknowledgements

Evelyn Cammon
(Editor)
Eve Cammon dreams of living in the tropics surrounded by books, both virtually and physically. She is absurdly grateful to have achieved the latter and gets closer to the former every day. If you want someone to love your book as much as you do, go look her up - www.readinkedits.net

Olegg Kulay-Kulaychuk
(Cover Illustrator/Designer)
Olegg does cool things with art. You can check him out at https://www.behance.net/olegg3d75

Made in the USA
Columbia, SC
19 March 2025